"5-Stars! A great read!" – Robert W. Busby, United States Dept. of Defense (Ret)

"James Miller does it again! Another great book in the Cody Musket series." – Carol from LA

"I could hardly put it down! I've enjoyed reading all of the books in this series. I would like to see another one" – Sheryl Young

"How amazing is Cody Jr! Like his father, like his mother, like his sister, following the call to save the children that fall into the hands of traffickers that enslave them." – Mabel Bossman

"An awesome story! Reading the lines filled me with an adrenalin rush, always holding my breath in anticipation for the next outcome . . . This book gives hope." – Martha Ngel

Books In This Series

  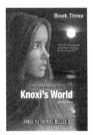

Land Without Shame

A Cody Musket Jr. Thriller
Book Four of the Cody Musket Series

James Nathaniel Miller II

Lions Tail
BOOKS™

Cover by Delaney_Design.com

Wordsmith
Proofreading

Printed and bound in the United States of America

INTRODUCTION

In the Musket tradition, *Land Without Shame* is a different kind of love story — one that involves courageous children, freedom fighters, natural disasters, lovers, and haters. A story that you will feel deeply, as I did when I was writing it.

Faith by adversity. Love by surprise.

If you like intense human drama, fast action, humor, romance, and rescue, you will love the debut of Cody Musket Jr.

This story takes place 22 years in the future. The science-fiction technologies depicted in this novel could likely be commonplace by that period, but the needs of mankind will be the same. The search for compassion and forgiveness, and the battle between good and evil are ongoing.

This novel supports traditional family
values but deals head-on with adult subjects
of domestic violence and human trafficking.
No sexually explicit content.

Life can be meaningless when one has
everything to live for, but nothing to die for.

1

NOSE DIVE

Caracas, 2041

Cody entered the terminal at Simon Bolivar Airport on a razor's edge. He turned up his collar and pulled his cap low over his eyes. Venezuela's international airport was among the most dangerous in the world.

He glanced over his shoulder repeatedly. His unexpected discovery of an abandoned infant in a downtown garbage dumpster several hours earlier had caused him to miss his covert rendezvous with his contact. By stopping for the child, he had called attention to himself. Now, he was a target.

He had managed to give his pursuers the slip by the thinnest of margins, but his close encounter had earned him a swollen cheek and bleeding lip. His pursuers were still on the hunt, and his commuter flight to Barcelona would not depart for another hour.

The airport was crowded, making it easier for him to disappear, but when he arrived at the check-in area for his flight, only a handful of passengers were waiting. One was an unusually tall man who eyed him carefully as he checked in.

The man had dark features and could have been from anywhere. People from every nation passed through this terminal. He seemed to be expecting Cody, judging from his expression, but his intentions, good or bad, were not discernable. Cody sat down on the opposite side of the waiting area and avoided eye contact by reading a magazine.

Cody had walked the streets of Caracas for nearly a week in the attempt to cultivate allies and create resistance against the cartels. Studies had concluded that Latin America was the bloodiest real estate on the planet, and that Caracas was the most dangerous city on the continent.

Having a famous father doesn't always win friends. Sometimes it makes enemies. Hence, the cloak and dagger. He was never so anxious to get out of a city.

When his flight was called, he was the first to board. He buckled his seatbelt and waited, keeping his head down while carefully scrutinizing every individual who boarded. Soon, the aircraft taxied to the appropriate runway and departed. Cody and the other 26 occupants were airborne.

He looked down upon the city of Caracas as the D'Veau 4000 Commuter jet lifted off and banked eastward. The flight to Barcelona, another Venezuelan seacoast city, was supposed to last an hour. The sun had just set and a wet blackness now engulfed the aircraft as it climbed upward into the dark, misty clouds.

The man sitting across the aisle from him extended his hand. "My name's Victor Casal. What's yours?"

Victor was tall and muscular, friendly, and wore a Texas Rangers baseball jersey with Adidas work-out pants and running shoes.

Cody shook his hand. "My name's Cody. Where are you from?"

"Oh, here and there. You getting off at Barcelona or staying on for the flight to Trinidad?"

"Barcelona." Cody's eyes constantly scanned the cabin for signs of trouble.

Victor looked toward the front of the plane. "You recognize that chick on row three? The hot one with the dark hair and shiny boots? That's Diamond Casper. She's here to film *Land Without Shame*. Gonna be a blockbuster, they say."

Cody stretched his neck to take a look. "Hmmm, I noticed she looked familiar when she walked in, but . . ."

"That sawed-off punk with the biceps sitting with her is 'er bodyguard. You don't mess with him, they say."

Cody sat back. "Who's *they?* You seem to put a lot of credence into what *they* say."

Victor crossed his arms. "So, what's your last name? You look nervous. You hidin' something?"

"I'm an American, Victor. I don't trust anybody. You want everyone to believe you're Venezuelan because of that ink on your elbow, but you talk like a native-born American. You're wearing American gear, but that bracelet on your left wrist is what some Latin American special ops personnel wear instead of dog tags. Let me guess; a fake serial number is engraved underneath? Who are you really?"

"Hmmm." Victor nonchalantly covered up the bracelet with his right hand.

Cody was wary of strangers in this "land without shame." Political despots had placed spies everywhere. Venezuela was in freefall. The last vestiges of democracy had long since been torn asunder by rival parties. Frequent assassinations and arrests of opposition leaders had become so commonplace that peasants hardly noticed anymore.

In all this, the homeless children had paid the steepest price. Every morning, "death coaches" made the rounds through downtown Caracas to rid the streets of its deepest shame — the bodies of children who had died during the night.

Victor leaned toward Cody and lowered his voice. "Okay, I know who you are, Cody. I'm *Deep Blue*. I was at the appointed place downtown, but you never showed. Been lookin' for you ever since. You're a hard guy to locate when you don't wanna be found. So, what happened to you?"

Cody studied him for a moment. "So . . . Deep Blue? What's that?"

Victor grinned and looked around just as Cody had done earlier, his shifting eyes scanning the cabin before answering.

"Your father is Cody Musket, the once-famous baseball player. Here, check this out." He pulled up his billfold and opened the flap. "See, I brought along one of his old baseball cards. Your face looks just like the one on this card."

"Those old cards aren't easy to get anymore," Cody said.

"Are you kidding?" he snickered. "I got mine by sending in a coupon off a box of Cocoa Puffs. So . . . they say you're a good pilot like your father. They say you're trained in martial arts and the use of firearms."

"*They say?* There you go again, Victor." Cody took a close look around, then spoke under his breath. "I got distracted. That's why I didn't make it to the rendezvous point."

"What kind of distraction? Some lady?"

"Later," Cody answered. "I'll tell you later."

"It's just as well," Victor said. "I was sent by *Thirsty Giant* to follow you — keep you safe. We all agree that Caracas isn't viable at this time for a Planned Childhood base. The politicos in the capital city have no sympathy for suffering kids. Barcelona is better. There are two individuals you need to meet in Barcelona."

Cody checked his watch. "We'll be there in forty minutes."

He noticed that Victor had the same habit of constantly observing the other passengers. Cody discreetly took another look around. Screen star Diamond Casper, the raven-haired beauty, was engaged in quiet conversation with two female companions and her chunky bodyguard. The mysterious tall man he had first seen in the waiting area was seated in the rear of the cabin. He nodded when Cody looked his way, but no one else in the aircraft would make eye contact.

Suddenly, the aircraft made a sharp turn northbound. The unexpected violent turn elicited screams from passengers. Next, the flight was subjected to severe turbulence which caused oxygen masks to deploy, and which brought some of the luggage crashing to the floor from the overhead compartments.

The panic was on. Screaming and crying continued as an apparent explosion blew the cockpit door and sent smoke belching into the passenger cabin. The aircraft went into a steep dive, causing everyone to become weightless for a few seconds. Two men and three women whose seatbelts had been unfastened came flying out of their seats and crashed into the ceiling.

The occupants had had no warning. Cody and Victor looked at each other, their faces wrenched by surprise and horror. Was it an attempted hijacking gone awry? A bomb? A missile?

Both men knew the first priority was to pull the aircraft out of its dive and restore level flight. Did the cockpit crew need help?

Cody and Victor slid toward the front, moving luggage and people out of the way. When they arrived at the cockpit door, the scene was worse than either of them could have imagined.

The pilot and copilot were bloody and unconscious, both still seated. An overhead control panel, the apparent source of the explosion, had been blown apart, jagged pieces of the metal and plastic now embedded in surrounding areas. Internal wiring, now loose, dangling, and uncovered, showered the two unconscious crewmen with sparks.

Cody reached over the pilot and took hold of the yoke. He yanked with all his strength but could not pull the D'Veau 4000 out of its dive. He felt for the autopilot disconnect switch on the yoke, but when he pushed the button, it did not restore manual control.

The aircraft broke out of the clouds still in a steep dive at only 3000 feet above the ocean waves. In a matter of seconds, the commuter would plunge to the bottom of the Caribbean Sea. Cody and Victor braced for the inevitable.

2

KEEP YOUR NOSE DOWN

Six hours earlier

Maria Fuentes' shaky voice echoed in the stairway. "Señor Cody, you must keep your nose down. I know you are trying to help, but we are just poor common people. If they see you here, they will kill us. You must leave! We are not fighters like you and we have already lost too much. *Por favor! Leave us alone!*" She shut the door, leaving him standing in the hallway.

The old, converted whorehouse was now home to eighteen families, all of whom were scared out of their wits. Fear had driven them to distrust everyone. They were typical of the people Cody had met in Caracas.

When he turned to walk back down the creaking wooden stairway, two hooded figures were waiting at the bottom. Both had prominent mustaches, but other facial features were hidden by the dark, shadowy hoods. These two individuals made the blond hair on the back of his neck stiffen up.

The words of Mrs. Fuentes replayed in his mind: *"If they see you here, they will kill us."*

The men at the bottom of the stairway were waiting for him. He knew it, but even if he could defend himself successfully, there would surely be repercussions against the Fuentes family. The game was on. "*Buenos tardes*, gentlemen!" He grinned as he moved down the steps toward them. "Can you help me? Uh . . . I'm from the USA, and the last time I was here the Vasquez girls lived in that apartment at the top of this here stairway. You got any idea what happened to 'em?"

The two tangos raised their heads but did not remove the hoods.

"*Woo-hoo!* I mean that younger one was hot like *smokin' fuego!* You savvy English? I mean, maybe I'm in the wrong place! Like, I sort of lit up the tavern last night, uh, wassa name o' that place? So maybe I can't remember too good. *Me loco in la cabeza, eh*?"

One of the tangos stepped into his path at the base of the stairs. "You are definitely in the wrong place, crazy Americano. Maybe we show you the way home, eh?"

"I—I didn't mean nothin'. I mean, I can pay you in US dollars if you can tell me what happened to the Vasquez girls."

The two men grabbed Cody, pushed him through the door, and threw him into the street. "Give us all your money, Americano, then go home and do not come back to our street or we break your legs and give your *pantelones* to the poor!"

"Okay, okay, just don't hurt me." Cody fumbled his hand into the side pocket of his cargos and produced a wallet with $100 cash. "Here, you—you can have it all. Just let me go, okay?"

The two men removed the cash. "It says here that you are Simon Spencer from Amarillo, Texas. Uh, where are your boots, *Tejano?*"

"I—I left 'em in Texas. All I have is these combers with holes in 'em."

The first man struck Cody across the face and knocked him down. The second kicked him in the midsection, then stomped his face into the concrete. "Do not come back, *pobre Tejano!* We will be watching for you."

Cody watched the two men walk away laughing. He picked up his fake ID and wiped the blood from his lip as he began walking the other direction. Someone would surely discover his real identity if he stayed in this town any longer.

He checked the time. He was scheduled to meet his contact, codename *Deep Blue,* in just twenty-five minutes. He had parked his rented GI Surplus Jeep nearby, but when he approached his vehicle, he noticed five more hooded figures standing next to it. No more playing games.

He turned and trotted down a side alley, planning to skip a street then take a cab to his appointment. That's when he heard a sound that stopped him in his tracks.

An infant child was screaming. He swiveled his head around attempting to locate the source of the cries. It was difficult to pinpoint because the empty buildings along the sides of the alley echoed the sound.

He shook his head, trying to rid himself of the cobwebs from being knocked to the ground moments earlier. This was a dangerous area and he had already stayed too long. Bad guys were waiting for him at his vehicle, and surely others would be on his trail by now. This tiny distress call represented but one child among hundreds whose panicked cries went unheeded in this city every day. Multitudes depended on the success of his mission. Should he stop to help this single infant and risk getting caught?

The words of his older sister Knoxi rolled over in his mind: "*Always be willing to stop for just one. You never know when the unlikeliest encounter might change the history of the world."*

Cody slowed down his thoughts and tuned his ears. The haunting cries continued. He followed them to a dumpster filled to the brim with garbage. He grabbed a wooden crate and used it to stand on as he began carefully removing the cardboard boxes, smelly open garbage bags, and other items from the large trash container.

Finally, after piling a heap of garbage on the ground, he saw a naked child lying amidst the filth near the bottom of the trash bin — a newborn, a baby boy, wearing no towel, no diaper, no blanket. The umbilical cord had been tied off with twine, but someone had thrown him away.

Cody took a cautious glance in every direction, then decided to lower himself into the dumpster. He carefully picked up the tiny boy. Now what?

He cradled the hungry child hoping to calm his cries and peeked out to see if anyone had noticed. The alley was deserted. He needed to call his father immediately to report in.

He hunkered down inside the dumpster, pulled out his old-style smartphone, and punched the number. The voice at the other end was obviously waiting for his call.

"Rosa's Cantina, this is Marty. Is the surf up?"

"Marty, this is Gunfighter. Surf is down. Repeat, surf down."

"Give me the details."

"Details as follows: Scheduled meeting not possible. In possession of hungry baby bird in peril. Need progressive route from these coordinates to nearest railroad."

"Copy that. Switch to tac M-1."

"Switching to tac M-1."

Cody called up the tactical M-1 App so that his father, Cody Senior, could link up and download the directions he had requested. He then cautiously climbed out of the odorous garbage bin, and immediately heard shouting.

The five-man crew which had surrounded his jeep was on to him. He began running as fast as his feet would carry him with the infant hidden underneath his shirt. The child began to cry again. Cody was blown.

When he reached the end of the alley, he turned left and fled down the street. He knew that within minutes a whole crowd of hoodies would be in pursuit of him and that he could expect help from no one in this community of fear. What were his options? He was determined. *There's no way anybody's gonna get this child!*

The next instant, he heard voices and guitar music. He came upon a crowd of people gathered for a mid-afternoon festival. A birthday party, maybe? A Venezuelan mariachi band was playing.

An elderly woman called out when she spotted him. "*Señor*, we have your hat and coat for you to try on!"

Cody was stunned. "Uh, *gracias, señora*." He caught his breath. "*Se ven como yo esperaba.*" ("They look exactly as I was expecting.")

He walked right into the bright, gala-striped coat she was holding open for him. He was careful to not drop the child in the process. She then placed a large straw sombrero on his head.

Cody mingled with the crowd, wearing the hat and coat until he saw his pursuers pass by unaware. He then returned the coat and hat to her. *"Muchas gracias señora. Que Dios esté contigo."* ("Thank you very much, ma'am. May God be with you.")

She smiled "You must work a little on your Spanish, my young friend." Then she moved closer. "And do not worry. The tiny treasure you protect with your life will be kept safe. There is Uber driver waiting for you if you walk through this door into my shop and come out in alley behind."

Cody walked through the tiny shop toward the back door, filled with thoughts of wonder. Was she a hero, or an angel? *Ha! Mom must be prayin' for me again.*

~   ~   ~

Fifteen minutes later, after taking a ride with Uber, he stood in front of the specified building. It was an old adobe dwelling. Once proud, the structure had been converted to a boarding house in this dilapidated section of town. But with colorful lights, arched windows, and a flat roof with flowers planted on top, it was obvious that someone took pride in appearances.

He knocked. An attractive early-fifties Venezuelan woman wearing a faded yellow apron cracked open the door. Her hair was dark with streaks of gray, and her deep brown eyes were swollen and bloodshot.

Cody swallowed hard. *"Uh, buenas tardes, Señora. ¿Dónde está la Cantina de Rosa?"* ("Good afternoon, ma'am. Which way to Rosa's Cantina?")

The woman hesitated and glanced up and down the street nervously before whispering, "Señor, we are looking for baby birds. Do you have any of those?"

"Solo tengo una, Señora. ¿Esta bien?" ("I have only one, ma'am. Is that sufficient?")

The woman widened the door opening. "Come in, come in."

She led Cody to a back room. "Welcome, Gunfighter. I'm Wild Raven. Just call me Raven. Let me have the little bird." She took the newborn from Cody. He was quiet, but still alive.

"Sorry I couldn't find a decent towel to wrap him in. I found him in a dumpster. I was runnin' for my life, couldn't stop. I just carried him under my shirt. Marty trusts you. That's good enough for me."

Just then, a young woman who appeared to be in her middle teens stood in the doorway. She immediately eyed the child affectionately.

"This is Maria Valentes," Raven said. "She just lost her baby, but she still has milk. She is in deep mourning, but has agreed to accept this child as a gift from God. I think you can see that she has already bonded with him."

Maria delicately took her new son into her frail arms, then opened her robe and allowed the child to nurse at her breast. She closed the robe and turned around to face Cody. She said not a word, but her weepy brown eyes and grateful smile were enough.

Cody had never considered himself an emotional individual like his father, but as the teen mother and tiny infant slipped out of the room and into their new life together, it took all his will to hold back tears. Not only was this his first infant to rescue, it was also the first he had ever held in his hands.

"I never . . . never realized how small they are, how innocent, helpless."

Raven reached out and placed her hand on Cody's cheek like a mother to a son. "Gunfighter, it is not a weakness for a man to cry. My husband is a doctor. He sees the pain every day. He cries every night."

Cody blinked several times.

"She will be a good mother," Raven said. "Maria is one that we rescued from *Los Torturadores.* She will be safely transported to Dominica in two days. She has been abused in unthinkable ways, and she did not want to leave here without her baby who is gone. But now, this child and mother can comfort each other."

Cody dropped his eyes and allowed himself a soft, measured smile.

"When you pulled that child out of the dumpster, Gunfighter, you saved two lives, not just one. And now the word has already spread through the underground. You have lifted us all to new courage and joy."

Cody cleared his throat. "So, do you often rescue abused girls like Maria?"

"We have eight more women here and three more coming in. We have not lost one yet. We eventually get them all to freedom. So far, our activities have not been discovered by the cartels. The government cannot protect us, so we pray every day we will not be exposed."

Cody was spellbound. He had met other heroic people since becoming a leader with "Rosa's Cantina," but this woman was something special.

"How long before your flight departs?" Raven asked.

Cody peeked at his watch. "I need to be at the airport in two hours."

"You know, Gunfighter, the baby did what was natural all over your clothes. At least his little body is working. Also, you smell like the garbage dumpster. I invite you to use my shower behind that curtain. The water does not get hot, only warm. Maria would be glad to wash and dry your clothes for you while you clean up. We can have you out of here in one hour."

"Ma'am, your hospitality is more than I expected. I'll hand you my clothes through the curtain."

"Good. I will hang a robe next to the shower. When you finish, you can wear the robe while we wait for Maria to finish your clothes. We will feed you a modest meal and arrange a safe ride to the airport. We know a driver."

"I don't know what to say." Cody smiled.

"My husband will be home soon to examine the child." She placed her warm hand on Cody's swollen left cheek. "I won't even ask what happened to your face, Gunfighter." She smiled. "The less I know, the better. My husband will have a look at your injuries when he arrives."

Cody entered the shower, nodded back to Raven, and closed the curtain.

3

LIFE AFTER DEATH

Cody and Victor had but seconds to live. The aircraft was plunging toward the ocean at nearly 500 knots. They could see the individual waves in the intermittent moonlight. They closed their eyes and braced for impact.

Suddenly, their senses were shocked as the aircraft inexplicably leveled itself off a few hundred feet above the water.

"What happened?" Victor panted, out of breath. "So is this what life after death is like?"

"I have no idea what happened or why, but we need to get these pilots out of their seats and somehow get control of this plane and point it toward land."

"Roger that," Victor said, his voice shaking. He cleared his throat. "Maybe there's a doctor on board. These two pilots . . ."

"Forget it," Cody said. "Pilot and copilot both dead. There's no pulse."

"We need to get the people calmed down," Victor pointed out. "We gotta see who on board can help. People are injured back there."

"Yeah, it's chaos. Help me move these guys." Cody pulled the pilot from the seat.

After they had placed the pilot and copilot in the floor of the passenger compartment, Victor addressed the passengers.

"Okay, please listen! *Okay, vale, por favor escucha!*"

Most of the passengers stopped to listen. Some were in tears. Victor explained that an unknown malfunction had caused the explosion, and that Cody was a trained pilot and was in two-way communications with Venezuelan flight controllers. He spoke in English and followed up with Spanish. He appealed to the passengers to remain calm and help the injured.

Meanwhile, Cody had his hands full. When Victor returned to the cockpit, Cody gave him an earful of bad news.

"I can't get anything back online. Every system is out of my control. We're headed out to sea and there's nothing I can do about it. I can't turn the plane or control the engine thrust. Even my cell phone is useless. No service."

"So what are our options?"

"Okay," Cody began. "First of all, I've never flown this type aircraft. I need the flight manual to figure out the systems. I'm not sure how much the explosion damaged the navigation components and avionics. We have no communications, no nav, no com. What's even scarier is that someone else seems to be controlling this aircraft."

"You mean like remote control?"

"Exactly. A moment ago while you were talking to the passengers, the aircraft banked left and picked up a three-hundred-forty-degree heading. It has followed that course without the slightest deviation ever since. Whoever is doing this knew exactly which systems to take out with that explosion to prevent anyone from regaining control or calling for help."

"Hmmm." Victor scratched his head. "Could it be someone on board? Someone using an electronic device?"

"Anything's possible."

"Look," Victor said. "I picked up the passenger manifest. Everyone on this list is either injured or out of their mind, except for one — the tall guy at the back. He seems relatively undisturbed."

"Is he Venezuelan?"

"Lemme look. It says his name's Joseph Parker, African American, age eighty-one. He's smiling, calm as ice water. Makes me suspicious."

"You should go question him. And show everyone how to put on the life preservers and tell 'em to remove their shoes."

After Victor left, Cody heard a voice behind him. "Would someone tell me what's going on? I mean . . . I was supposed to be somewhere. I knew I shouldn't have ridden on this cheap airline. This cheap plane!"

Cody looked back. "Hello, Ms. Casper. You might show some respect. You're practically standing on the dead bodies of two crewmen."

"Do you even know who I am? I have a movie to make. I demand you get me there! Why are cell phones and holocoms not working? And what happened to your face? Did she beat you up last night?"

"I'm only gonna give you one chance to make yourself useful, Diamond. Get in here, sit down, and fasten your seatbelt. Now!"

"Who do you think you are? Who in hell do you think you are!"

"I'm not anybody in Hell, Diamond. But . . . I'm somebody in Heaven."

"I'm speechless."

"No need to say anything," Cody said. "Either get in here and sit down, or go back to your seat."

Diamond hesitated, then moved forward and took a seat in the copilot chair. "Okay, I'm here. Now what?"

"Fasten your seatbelt."

She coupled her seatbelt. "I'd rather ride up here anyway. Everybody back there either threw up or soiled their pants. Can you imagine the smell?"

"I need to find the flight manual. It should be in the bulkhead behind your chair. Can you swivel around and look for it?"

"So . . . so what does it look like? Oh, wait. I think I found it."

~   ~   ~

At the rear of the passenger compartment, Victor found Joseph Parker stooping over an injured flight attendant. She had told him how to access the first-aid kit. He was dressing her head wound.

"Mr. Parker? I wonder if I might have a word with you."

"Certainly, sir. Anything else I can do, just let me know. I almost have this lady fixed up. She's gonna need a hospital."

"You seem to know what you're doing."

"I was a US Navy corpsman. Served in Afghanistan. Saw plenty of wounds like this. She'll be okay, but she needs more than I can give her here. I have a message for the young man flying this airplane. That's Cody Musket's son, isn't it?"

Victor made his voice quiet. "How do you know that, sir?"

"I'm from Hondo, Texas. Everybody down there knows the Muskets."

"Okay, Mr. Parker, but —"

"Please, young man, call me Joe."

"Okay, uh, Joe. What's your message for Cody?"

"Tell him I am askin' Jesus for a miracle, and I know that God will somehow bring good from all that has happened. Tell him not to worry, because Satan will eventually overplay his hand."

Victor frowned. "I'll give him the, uh, message. I don't want to interrupt your good work here."

Victor left Parker with the flight attendant, determined to keep a close watch on the old man. When he returned to the cockpit, he was surprised to see Diamond Casper sitting next to Cody. She was crying.

"I leveled with Diamond about our situation," Cody said. "I think she's taking it well. We located the manual, but it would take me days to figure out all these emergency procedures. Besides, we have no way to restore manual control to this plane."

"How long have we been on the three-forty heading?"

"About thirty minutes," Cody responded.

Just then, the aircraft banked to the right and turned to a heading of forty degrees.

"Here we go again," Cody said. "Somebody is manipulating this whole event. What about the guy you questioned?"

"I just looked back there. He's still helping the flight attendant with a head injury. He has his hands full. He couldn't have manipulated the course change."

"Unless it was all pre-programmed," Cody said.

"Uh," Victor breathed heavily. "He said Satan always overplays his hand, and he's backin' you with prayers to Jesus, or something like that."

"*Ohhh!* That's good to know," Diamond snickered. She wiped her face with her shaking hand, determined to not cry again. "God must be punishing me for not ever going to church. I never learned anything about that stuff." She blotted her eyes with her sleeve. "And now, here we are."

"Whoever's doing this is going to a lot of trouble," Cody said. "This is a remote hijacking. Somehow, this hacker managed to circumvent all the safeguards. Can you think of any reason why someone would use a method like this to abduct you?"

"Me? You think I'm the cause?"

"What about the movie you were gonna film in Venezuela?"

"You mean *Land Without Shame?* I play the part of a woman brought to shame who rises above it to bring back law and order. It's a good part, but I'm not *that* person; not at all. I just wanna live in Malibu and make movies. Acting is my life."

"So, you're not a freedom fighter after all?"

"I leave that to others. It isn't my fault that people can't provide for themselves. So, what's your name, anyway?"

"Name's Cody."

"Cody what? I mean, what's your last name?"

"Just . . . just Cody."

"Well, Cody . . . just Cody. How in hell . . . I'm sorry. I—I mean how can you be so composed? Cuz, like, we're in a plane you don't know how to fly, on our way to who knows where! We're over the ocean in the middle of the night, we don't know who's behind this, and at any second we could go into another crash dive!"

She stared into his face. "I mean, my bodyguard — "Crusher" we call him — he's the bravest man I know, and he's glued to his seat, flexing his biceps by squeezing the life outta the armrests! How can you be so . . . so together?"

Cody looked into her deep ebony eyes for the first time. "You have a cut above your left eye."

His response clearly caught her off guard. Had he not heard

a word she had said? Or, perhaps she wasn't used to men looking directly into her eyes except when acting.

She softened. "So . . . do they really know you in Heaven? I figure *everybody* knows me. 'Cept I dunno spit about Heaven. So, like, is that why?" She fought tears again. "Is that why you're so freakin' calm?"

4

KEEP THE NOSE UP

Cody and Diamond finally ran out of words. With shaking hands, Diamond reached back and pulled paper wipes out of the cabinet behind her. She used them to clean streaks of blood off the copilot yoke in front of her. Cody began tapping his fingers on the pilot yoke as he watched the fuel quantity dwindle to a critical stage.

They had also observed lightning in the distance, the flashes getting closer and closer.

Diamond tried not to notice Cody's nervous fingers. Perhaps he wasn't as fearless as she had thought.

"We have about forty-five minutes of fuel left," Cody said. "We're approaching ten o'clock. We've been on a forty-degree heading for over two hours. That's gonna put us out to sea aways. I have no GPS, no way to pinpoint our position, and I can't call anyone."

"People will be looking for us though, right?" Diamond begged for Cody's assurance. She received none.

"I . . . well, of course. They'll send planes out to search. Probably at first light in the morning."

"You're not very convincing Mr. Cody, just Cody. And besides that, what do these people want with us?"

"I wish I knew. I'm not gonna sugar-coat it."

"Cody, if we had met under normal circumstances, I would never have even noticed you. Something tells me that you're not trying to save this plane just for yourself."

As she stared at the side of his face, the engines throttled back, the yoke moved forward slightly, and the aircraft began to lose altitude.

Diamond's mouth was so dry, her tongue so swollen, that she could hardly articulate. "What happened? Are we . . . are we going to c-crash?" She held her ears and shut her eyes.

Even through her closed eyelids, she could see a sudden flash of lightning. The airplane shuddered. Both engines lost power, and went silent.

"*Hold on!*" she heard Cody shout. "Keep the nose up! Keep the nose up!"

The next instant, she was thrown forward, restrained only by her seatbelt as the nose of the aircraft contacted the surface of the water.

The plane went airborne again for a few seconds, then banked right. When the right wing hit the water, the aircraft spun sideways and broke into pieces. The noise was deafening, grisly. Metal rivets popping, bulkheads breaking apart. Passengers screaming.

Then all was quiet except for the bubbling, choking sounds.

Diamond coughed and gurgled as rushing, cold saltwater swelled over her head and face. Instinct told her to swim upward, but she forgot how to unfasten the seatbelt. The sinking airplane was pulling her down. She was going to die. Then, she felt two arms free her from the belt and pull her from the wreckage.

A heartbeat later, she opened her eyes. She was lying face down on a sandy beach. It was night. Her eyes burned, but she could make out two women in white dresses walking barefoot away from her. She tried to call out but could make no sound. She blinked twice, then recognized them as her two traveling companions — Tige and Betsy, her manager and executive producer. But why were they walking away as if in a daze?

She raised her head and tried to turn over, but had not the strength. As her senses returned, she could hear distant thunder, rolling surf, and someone call for help. She felt waves gently washing over her feet.

"Are you okay, Ms. Casper?"

The voice was unfamiliar. She turned her head to look. It was a lanky, dark figure with an amiable smile, wearing no shirt.

"I'm Joe Parker, ma'am. Cody pulled you free from the plane and deposited you here. Are you hurt?"

Diamond tried to talk again. "I don't think I'm injured," she rasped. "You say someone pulled me from the plane? So . . . what happened? Where am I?"

"Ma'am, the plane crashed. Cody and I have been looking for more survivors all night. Just rest now."

"The . . . the plane? Oh, yeah. I remember. Where's Cody? How did I get on this beach? What time is it? What's wrong with my shoulder?"

No one answered. She looked the other direction and saw a familiar figure moving slowly toward her. "Cody . . ." She called out to him weakly.

But Cody seemed oblivious. He took a few more steps, dropped to his knees, and finally collapsed face down on the sand about twenty feet away.

She dragged herself to where Cody lay, stroked his sandy hair To get his attention, then restd her head in the center of his back and succumbed to her own exhaustion.

~   ~   ~

Diamond awoke just as the first rays of dawn hit her face. Cody was breathing heavily but had not moved a muscle. She tried to pull herself together as she stood to her feet and looked around.

The crash site was gruesome. The cockpit of the D'Veau 4000 lay on its side in shallow water less than 100 meters from the beach. A quarter mile farther offshore, the top of the tail was visible sticking out above the water.

The pilot and copilot were floating face down near the shoreline, and she counted five additional bodies washed up on the beach. Carry-on baggage and pieces of loose clothing littered the water and bobbed gently as morning waves rolled in.

She spotted Mr. Parker lying shirtless in the sand several yards away. She saw no one else other than Cody. Where was everyone? Weren't there 27 passengers and crew on board? Would they find other bodies? How many were alive? She remembered seeing Tige and Betsy walking on the beach earlier, but they were nowhere to be found. What about Crusher, her bodyguard?

She was standing alone in a nightmare. She had never been so scared. She wanted to run over and wake Cody, but that would have been selfish. He had spent most of the night looking for survivors, according to Mr. Parker. Cody needed to rest. But since when was she so concerned about being selfish?

What beach was this? Was this another continent or an island? Were there natives here? Headhunters? Witchdoctors?

Who was responsible for bringing down the plane? Why was Joe Parker shirtless?

"I see you made it through the night. How's your shoulder?"

The voice startled her. She turned around to see Cody walking toward her.

"Cody! You startled me. Uh . . . my shoulder?"

"Your left shoulder," Cody said. "We had to stitch and bandage it last night."

She felt her left shoulder and suddenly realized she was wearing Joe Parker's *Hunter Woods* designer dress shirt.

"Why am I wearing this shirt? Where's my blouse?"

"I pulled you through the cockpit escape window. Your blouse got caught on some stubborn Plexiglas and some jagged metal. I had to tear the blouse off you to get your head above water. You have a deep cut on your shoulder and a lotta lacerations on your, uh, midsection. Parker stitched you up and put his own shirt on you after we got you to shore. Somehow, he managed to salvage the med kit from the plane."

She stared through unsettled eyes. "What are we gonna do, Cody? Does anyone even know where we are? I guess it's a good thing I wore my white Honey Bear bikini top underneath."

Joe Parker walked into the conversation. "Do you mind if I have a look at your wounds, young lady? It was dark last night when I treated you."

"Mr. Parker, I can't wear your shirt. I-I've been a lot of trouble for you. I've never had someone literally give me the shirt off their back."

Cody spoke again. "I'll gather some of these bags while he examines your shoulder. You can find a blouse in one of them. I might even be able to find your carry-on. We need to bring these few floating bodies to shore and burn them as soon as we can, but that'll have to wait." Cody left to gather up the floating luggage.

"Mr. Parker, do you know how many men would pay a killer price to see me model a bikini . . . or less? But this guy, Cody, he just walks away. Is he gay or does he just think he's being a gentleman?" She began removing Parker's shirt.

"I think it's called respect — giving you some space. Besides, we're in crisis mode here. He has things to do."

"So, who is this guy Cody? What does he do? He wouldn't even tell me his last name. Is he hiding something?"

"I have said a prayer for that young man every day of his life, and yet he doesn't even know me."

"Continue," she said. "Please."

"Cody is involved in dangerous work. If he didn't reveal his identity, it was for a good reason."

"You mean he's like . . . like a spy? A CIA hitman maybe? I mean, you should have seen him last night. We were all losing it, and he wasn't even scared."

"Oh, he was plenty scared. But Cody's in the business of saving people, not killing them. When he gets to know your heart, he'll tell you who he is. I'm sure of it."

"Do you think anyone's looking for us, Mr. Parker?"

"I couldn't say."

"What about all the dead people? Did anyone else survive? Did you or Cody see my bodyguard last night? And what about the two women who were with me? Did you see them?"

"No, ma'am. It was nearly impossible to find anyone last night. The crash area was so large, and there was a terrible storm. Cody and I nearly drowned."

"Do you know who was responsible for the crash? Do you have any idea what they might want? Do you think they were just trying to kill us?"

"I wish I could tell you, ma'am."

When Cody returned several minutes later, Parker was wearing his own shirt again. Diamond was sitting on a log nearby looking at the wound on her shoulder.

She looked up and noticed that Cody had found her carry-on bag. "I've been watching you, Cody, just Cody. How did you find my bag?"

"Just a guess. It says 'Sweet Ebony' on it. That's you, isn't it?"

"You almost smiled, Mr. Cody. So you think it fits? Sweet Ebony?"

Cody looked toward her feet. "Hmmm, hope you have some shoes in the bag. We need to get off this beach and find shelter inland. The nearby terrain could be rough on bare feet."

"So then, if you'll hand me my bag, I'll find my tennis shoes and pullover shirt." She displayed a teasing grin, but lost the smile when she caught sight of the two dead pilots again.

Parker exchanged glances with Cody while he handed Diamond her bag.

"My friends call me Di," she said as she began searching through her clothes. "*Ugh!* Everything in here is soaked."

"It fits," Cody mumbled as he turned to walk away. "The title on your bag — *Sweet Ebony.*"

"Cody, you don't really have to leave. I was only . . ."

"Yes, I do. Parker and I need shoes, and we need to salvage whatever else we can from the luggage in the water. Finding food may not be an easy task either. We need to explore and see what this place offers."

5

SHALLOW WATER, HIGH GROUND

Cody and Parker gathered luggage from the water and began placing it on the beach while Diamond went through her bag looking for something to wear. She found a pullover blouse and put it on.

"How does this look, gentlemen? I prefer the bikini top, but since you boys obviously know nothing about finer things, I'll just wear it underneath."

Cody set another small bag on the sand, then commented, "This sun can be brutal. The pullover shirt gives more protection."

"That's all you think about, Cody? Protection? Who cares at a time like this? You're just afraid to look at me, that's all." She bit her lip and frowned. "Listen to me . . . talking trash and acting this way with death all around us. I should be ashamed."

A moment later, Cody glanced toward her. She was sitting on the sand sobbing. He ambled over to her and knelt on one knee. "We could use your help, Di. There's a lotta luggage to bring ashore." He left and went back to work.

After a few minutes, Diamond waded into the shallow water. "Okay," she said. "What do you want me to do?"

"Search through these bags after we lay them on the beach. Look for anything we might need, like shoes, food, anything we can take inland to help us survive."

When two hours had passed, they were exhausted again. The adrenaline rushes the night before had left them depleted.

Due to stress, they had not been hungry, but Cody knew that food was a priority. He found himself wondering what had happened to his friend Victor. Had he survived somehow? What about the others?

"I know we're tired, but we have to keep moving," Cody said. "I see dark clouds to the north. We could have more storms tonight. We need to look for shelter."

Suddenly, Diamond sounded an alarm. "Look! Someone's coming!"

"It's Victor!" Cody shouted, running toward the staggering figure.

Victor stumbled sideways into the shallow water just as Cody got to him. "Are you hurt?"

"Uh . . . no," Victor panted. "I searched all night for others. Couldn't find anyone. I found a shallow cave to crash in, but didn't sleep."

The temporary relief revitalized Cody. "I wondered about you. Parker and Diamond Casper are with me. We're the only survivors so far."

Victor held on to Cody as they staggered along. "Listen," Victor said. "I heard voices this morning." He ran short of breath. "I dunno. Maybe I was just hearing things, but they sounded like several men and some women. One guy was shouting, threatening the others. I didn't think the cave was safe anymore, so . . . so I came this direction."

"Glad you did. We need to put our heads together, figure things out."

"I saw a beached shark just beyond the bend." Victor took another deep breath. "Small one, 'bout three feet long. The storm must have brought it ashore last night. It was still flopping around early this morning. The meat might still be good if the crabs don't get there first."

When Victor and Cody joined the others, Diamond was eating a chocolate bar. "Help yourselves, gentlemen. I found two boxes of these in one of the carry-ons."

"Bravo," Cody said. "Listen, everybody. Victor found a fresh beached shark around the bend. If we can find a knife somewhere, we can have steaks tonight. Yeah, that is, if we can start a fire."

"Couldn't bring a knife aboard a commercial flight," Victor pointed out. "We'll have to either get creative or dive into the cargo hold and see what's down there, but . . ."

"Impossible," Cody said. "It's under forty feet of water."

Diamond noticed the obvious. Victor was in his boxer shorts. "What happened to your britches?"

"I had to ditch the baggy jeans. They slowed me down too much in the water. Thought I was gonna drown during the storm."

"What size you need, *Sharkman*? We found plenty o' pants earlier. Lemme guess. Thirty-four waist? And, judging by those feet, size eleven."

Victor was still trying to get his breath. "Sounds close enough, ma'am."

Cody glanced out at the distant lightning. "We need to find shelter. What about the voices you heard? Do you think you were followed?"

"I . . . I dunno. I left the cave and stayed inside the tree line as much as I could 'til I reached the bend. That's when I saw you coming to get me. I suggest we find a similar cave on higher ground up that ridge over there. That'll put us near enough to keep an eye on the wreckage in case someone shows up. It should also keep us above any huge swells from the storm."

"What if we don't find a cave?" Diamond wanted to know.

Victor had the answer. "Shouldn't be hard to find one. The cave I found earlier was an old lava tube. If there's one, there could be others. We must've crashed near a dormant volcano."

"Okay," Cody said. "Our first priority is to find a secluded shelter from the storm. We aren't sure about the voices Victor heard, but someone could be hunting us. We need to hide. Gather up all the chocolate bars and containers to catch rainwater. We'll have to leave the shark to the crabs."

~ ~ ~

Cody, Diamond, Victor, and Parker trudged up the hill watching for snakes, spiders, and other dangerous critters. They encountered plenty of mosquitoes and flies, but they saw no birds or other wildlife. The terrain began with a gentle slope, then became steeper and steeper as they climbed. There were obstacles to deal with such as loose volcanic rocks, boulders, branches, and thorns. Joe Parker proved to be more agile than the others had expected, even while carrying his share of supplies from the luggage.

Immediately upon reaching the ridge, they stumbled upon a cave which twisted and turned deeply into the hillside. The large entry was nearly hidden by tropical palm leaves, vines, branches, and rocks. It was unoccupied and showed no tell-tale signs of animals or humans.

The cave was a large lava tube, formed by molten lava that had cooled and left a tunnel. It was an extraordinary find. Lava tubes had no stalagmites or stalactites as in the more slowly-formed caves.

The surfaces in this cavernous sanctuary were smooth, even slick in places. The bottom of the main tube was flat, making it easier on bare feet, and featured formations that could serve as benches and pedestals — a common characteristic of these natural caves.

The "ceiling" was rounded — arched — as if someone had designed it that way.

Victor sat down on a ledge just inside the entrance. "This place looks ideal. Must be another opening somewhere. Feel that draft? Great for building a fire. The draft will pull the smoke out. I also hear water dripping. There must be a hole above where the rainwater came through last night and pooled someplace." He breathed heavily and leaned back against the rocky wall.

Parker spoke up. "Why were you limping, Victor? You're favoring that right leg. Better let me take a look."

"I wrenched my knee somehow last night during the crash. This climb may have aggravated it."

Diamond nonchalantly pulled aside a palm branch and peeked down at the crash site. She gasped. "Take a look at this!" She motioned with her hand for Cody to hurry.

Cody moved quickly to the cave opening and looked down toward the beach. "Do you know those people?" He kept his voice down. "Three men and two women."

"Yes! That's my bodyguard Crusher with Tige and Betsy. They

are alive! But those other two guys have guns!"

Everyone gathered at the opening and watched. One of the individuals holding a weapon was becoming animated. It was difficult to hear the conversation, but things were getting ugly. Finally, the gunman pointed his weapon at one of the women. Crusher charged into him and wrestled the handgun away, but the other tango drew a weapon and shot Crusher in the chest. Crusher wasn't finished. He charged the shooter and tackled him. Another shot was fired but it was difficult to determine from which gun it had originated.

The tackled shooter got up, but Crusher stayed down motionless. The two men put ropes around the women's wrists and began leading them away.

Diamond tried to break through the leaves and run down the hill, but Cody restrained her. He muffled her angry cries with his right hand over her mouth and pulled her back to the seclusion of the cave. She slapped him and scratched his right arm, twisting and screaming, the veins in her neck bulging and turning red.

"Di, please stop fighting me. It won't help Crusher or your two friends if you go down there. Do you understand?"

Her body writhed and she began to sob. He released her. She pushed him back and turned away. "Leave me alone! Somebody needs to go down there to help Crusher."

Diamond began to hyperventilate. "I have never . . . I mean, I've made movies. I've even been shot in films, but . . ."

Victor spoke up. "Real life's different. You can't know until you've experienced it. We can't go down there until the two bad guys are out of sight. We're unarmed."

"You gotta slow down your breathing, Di. You're gonna pass out," Cody told her.

Di turned around. "Please. We have to rescue Tige and Betsy. We can't just stand here. If someone doesn't go, I'll do it myself."

Cody held firm, but softened his eyes. "Last night, you told me that you prefer to leave the rescuing to others. I take it you've changed your mind." He paused for a sigh. "Welcome to my world."

Diamond said nothing, unable to prevent fresh tears from rolling down her pampered cheeks. Her trial by saltwater, followed by a night on the beach, followed by the shooting of an associate in broad daylight, had stolen the CoverGirl glow from her face.

Cody turned and looked down at the beach again. "They've gone. C'mon Joe, let's see if we can help that wounded man down there."

Victor jumped up, "Lemme get my shoes on."

Cody stopped him. "You gotta stay here, Victor. Joe and I will check out Crusher, then I'm going after the women alone. Your knee will just slow me down."

Di grabbed Cody by the arm. "You're going after Tige and Betsy? I'm coming with you. I won't slow you down, and I won't take *no* for an answer." She followed him down the hill. "Cody, are you listening?"

When they reached the bottom, Crusher was still alive. After Parker examined his wounds, he whispered quiet words into the ear of the dying bodyguard.

Diamond began to cry again, then clenched her jaws together. "I promised myself I wouldn't lose it."

Crusher looked up at Cody with a rattle in his throat. "I . . . I didn't tell 'em anything. Your description, your identity. I told 'em you were black and looked like a fairy." He grinned, then coughed.

"They were gonna kill me anyway. I saw their operation. Child laborers . . ." He stopped when he saw Di's face. "I'm sorry I got myself killed, Di. I couldn't protect Betsy and Tige."

Cody knelt next to Crusher. "Child laborers? What product were they producing?" Cody waited. "Crusher, can you hear me?"

Crusher's eyes darkened. He whispered, "I picked his pocket after he shot me. I stole this." He pulled a mini handgun from underneath his shirt. "His backup weapon." He closed his eyes. "G'bye . . . Di." He was gone.

Cody solemnly stood to his feet. "Being afraid in an airplane doesn't mean a man's a coward."

Diamond stood in shock, but she recovered quickly. "I'm going with you. You can't say *no* to me."

"I absolutely will not let you go, Diamond Casper."

"Then don't go, Cody. You don't stand a chance. You're gonna just get yourself killed. How old are you anyway, eighteen?"

"I've trained for this with my father's organization since I was thirteen. I've already been on several missions. I have the element of surprise and I'm a good tracker. This is what I do. It's like . . . like a calling."

"But what if I'm telling you goodbye for the last time? What's a calling worth then?"

"All I can tell you is that if I stay here knowing what Tige and Betsy are facing, I could never live with it."

"Now that makes no sense. No sense at all. Why do you care about two people you've never met?"

Cody placed the gun under his belt. "I need to get a move on. They have a fifteen-minute head start, but they're moving slow with two barefoot women with ropes around their wrists. I'll have no problem catching up."

"I'm coming with you! That's final!"

Parker and Cody briefly glanced at each other.

Cody took hold of Diamond's shoulders. "Diamond Casper, don't make me restrain you."

An acquiescent smile emerged through her tears. "Cody, just Cody, at least tell me who you are. Please, I have to know before you go."

"Name's Musket. Cody Musket." Cody loosened his grip.

She tilted her head, obviously not recognizing the name, then she slowly stepped forward and wrapped her arms around his neck, shut her eyes, moved her lips close to his, and kissed him. When she opened her eyelids, Cody's face was as stiff as Stone Canyon.

She placed her hands on his chest. "Forgive me, Mr. Musket. I've never kissed a man who actually cared about me, or cared about my friends. I . . . just wanted to know what it felt like."

Diamond reached down and pulled off her shoes. "Put my shoes in your back pocket and grab the other pair over by that suitcase. It's the last pair we've found so far. Don't you bring back my friends with no shoes on their feet. Is that clear?"

"Yes, ma'am."

~   ~   ~

Diamond and Parker started back up the hill. Di kept glancing back toward the departing Cody, whose image grew smaller and smaller as he trotted away toward his deadly rendezvous.

"Mr. Parker, who the heck is Cody Musket?"

"Have you not heard the Musket name before? Cody Musket

Senior casts a long shadow, but Cody Jr. is building a legacy of his own, and most of it is done in secret. He's twenty-two by the way, same as you."

"I've heard of Knoxi Musket, but not Cody."

"Cody is Knoxi's younger brother."

"Never heard of him. Too bad Cody's gonna die today. We might've become . . . friends. Crusher is already dead because of me."

"Listen, Ms. Casper, there was no talking Cody out of going after your friends. He needs to go, and we need to pray."

"Pray? You expect me to pray? I never do that. Who do you pray to?"

"Perfect time to learn, madam."

"So, you think if we pray for Cody's safety, some god will answer us?"

"I am not concerned about Cody's safety. I'm prayin' for the two men he's gonna catch in a few minutes. Lord have mercy."

After she and Parker climbed back to the ridge, both glanced back toward the beach once more before entering the cave. Once inside, Victor greeted them.

"Sorry about your bodyguard, Ms. Casper. He must've been a good man. Later, we need to gather all the bodies together and burn them. Maybe Parker will say some words over them. I'm not a religious man, but I still believe in respect."

"Call me Di. Cody already mentioned about the bodies. We can't leave 'em lyin' around. I still think I'ma wake up tomorrow and find out this is all just a bad dream."

She walked toward the back of the cave and sat down, then lowered her head and began to sob again.

Parker grabbed a chocolate bar and peeled off the wrapper,

then walked toward her, saying, "I'm going to walk a ways and explore. Maybe there's another exit."

"I wanna come with you." She dried her eyes with her hands. "I need . . . I mean, I've gotta be busy."

"C'mon, young lady, let's go exploring. Do you mind if I put my arm around you as we walk?"

She looked into Parker's seasoned face. "*Ohhh*, I wish someone would. No one ever wants to put an arm around these shoulders unless they want something costly in return. Careful for my stitches."

"No worries, I'll be careful. By the way, I think Cody appreciated that kiss more than you know."

She stopped and threw both her arms around him and began crying again. "Mr. Parker, I'm *so* scared. I can't help myself. I've just watched one good man die. I wish I could believe Cody will return, but that's too much to hope for. Besides, I mean, he never gave me a straight answer about why he risked his life for my two friends. And there's a storm coming. What if he gets caught in the rain somewhere out there and . . . and gets, like, disoriented, and can't find his way back, or something like that?"

"Now listen to me, Diamond. Cody has been through extensive training, both spiritually and mentally. The Musket family has a motto: '*When you're doing God's work, dying is something you can live with.*'"

"Ugh! That makes no sense, and it scares me. Does he want to be a martyr or something like that? Does he have a death wish?"

"No, but that's why he went after your friends. He considers it God's work."

They started walking again. "Diamond, when Cody was just

thirteen, he began preparing himself — weapons, self-defense, endurance, articles of faith. When he was eighteen, he tested his own mettle with the same wilderness survival test that Navy SEALs endure. He was released alone in the wilderness with only a knife — no food, no drinking water, and a five-man SEAL team hunting him." Parker stopped for a deep breath, then continued.

"He lived strictly off the land. It took them seven days to capture him. They threw him stripped naked into a six-foot hole and covered the top of it with bars. He sat at the bottom of that hole with his hands and feet tied for seven hours, after which they pulled him out and interrogated him with body blows and fists to the face."

"Stop, stop. I had no idea."

Parker was undeterred. "Finally, they untied him and brought in a woman bound with ropes. She was an actress, like you. Five SEALs began a simulated assault on the lady, and told Cody he was free to go. He was so depleted he couldn't separate reality from make-believe. He pretended to leave, and a minute later, he doubled back and charged into the room from the other side. He managed to temporarily free the actress from the five SEALs before they could corral him."

Diamond frowned. "So . . . so did Cody go to the hospital? I mean with all his injuries —"

"Oh, yes. He spent two days recovering, as did two of the SEALs. A week later, the SEAL team took him and the woman downtown and treated them each to a $200 steak dinner."

"Why would an eighteen-year-old man go through all that?"

"Because the SEAL survival exercise will show a young warrior precisely what his capabilities are and exactly where his limits lie. After having gone through this test, Cody will not overestimate himself, nor will he underestimate an enemy. And because of his faith, he fears no man."

"How do you know so much about Cody?"

"Well, let's just say I make it my business to know certain things."

She fought back tears. "Mr. Parker, do you think I will know it when he . . . I mean, will I feel it the moment he . . ."

"The moment he dies? You sense a connection to him, don't you, young lady," Parker concluded.

"I shouldn't have kissed him. What was I thinking? He must think I'm a real piece of art." She shook her head. "I hate myself."

"Cody isn't gonna be killed today, Di, and about that kiss—"

"Mr. Parker, if only you had been my father. Maybe . . . maybe my life would have been so different."

"Are your parents still living?"

She wiped tears from her face. "There are certain things I can never talk about with anyone. We all have secrets, right?" She passed him a skeptical glance. "For example, it wasn't just dumb luck that put you on that flight, Mr. Parker. There's much you aren't telling me."

"Hmmm," Parker said. "I feel a strong draft. We must be coming to an opening in this cave somewhere back here."

"Mr. Parker, Joe, what do you believe happens to us when we die? Isn't that your business too?"

Parker smiled.

6

THE GUY WHO GETS THE GIRL

Cody followed the tracks of the two killers who had taken Diamond's friends. The men had killed Crusher in cold blood. He had seen it himself. What should he do with them? He had two courses of action: He could kill them and attempt to hide the bodies, or he could take them alive to the cave as prisoners. If he let them go, they would blow his cover. That was not an option.

The best course was to capture and interrogate them. But would they talk? They were plenty brave killing an unarmed bodyguard, but how hardened would they be without weapons or backup? How much did they believe in their cause, whatever that was? Were these guys the leaders, or just hirelings?

Eventually, the tracks turned off the beach and into the jungle. He would need to keep his eyes peeled for ambushers waiting in the trees ahead.

Cody moved swiftly inside the tree line and hunkered down. Out of breath, he reached into a pouch he had brought along and pulled out a small, cell-powered listening device. He turned it on and put the earbud into his right ear.

He could hear their footsteps. The small screen told him the sounds came from only forty-seven meters away. They were on foot, heading 27 degrees from north. He reached back into the pouch and pulled out his shepherd's sling, a model of the very device carried by some ancient warriors as a backup weapon, and the device the teenaged David had used to protect his father's sheep ranch from predators and to kill the Nephilim giant Goliath, champion of the Philistine army, in the Valley of Elah.

The sling was effective from short range and silent enough that it would not alert other hostiles in the area. He pulled up four friction-formed rocks he had obtained from the banks of the Brazos River in Central Texas. He was well-armed with his sling, a small handgun, and the element of surprise. The gun was not the best option, because the sound might attract unwanted additional combatants.

Like David, Cody had practiced relentlessly with the sling, and he had become adept. He could routinely destroy a perfectly good grapefruit at a distance of ten yards.

He heard no other footsteps within range of the listening device so he moved forward cautiously, listening all the while. Cody finally spotted them moving upward toward a clearing on the side of a slope. If they reached the clearing, he would lose the advantage. The time to act was now. They were moving single-file over a well-travelled but narrow trail. The two women were in the middle, with one hostile in front and the other in back. His first target would be the trailer.

He placed his pouch on the ground, slid his shepherds sling under his belt, and moved rapidly but quietly ahead until he was directly behind his target. He easily disabled the first tango with a chokehold which left the individual unconscious on the ground. No one noticed that the trailer was down, not even the women.

He made a quick move forward and wrapped his arms around

the woman who was next in line, placing his hand over her mouth, pressing hard so she could make no sound.

"Don't say a word," Cody whispered into her ear. "I'm not gonna hurt you. I'm here to help."

She gave him a frantic nod.

Then, Cody could see his plan unraveling. The second woman looked back. When she saw Cody, she stopped in her tracks, which alerted the other hostile.

Cody pulled up his sling and a rock, anticipating the worst. "Get down, Betsy!" he yelled as he whipped the rock forward, striking the malefactor in the chest before he could draw his gun.

Cody wrestled the stunned individual to the ground, applying the same chokehold and achieving the same result as the first. Both killers were down and both woman were huddled together, alternately looking at each other and staring at Cody. Cody confiscated all weapons and pulled the headsets off the hostiles, hoping that neither had been able to alert anyone.

That's when he noticed something that gave him chills. Both women were wearing electro-shock collars.

"Ma'am, let me look at this collar."

"Uh, who are you?" she blurted. "How did you know my name was Betsy? Have we ever met?"

"Just a guess, ma'am. I can't get this collar off. I'm gonna have to get one of these men to give me the combination."

Cody rapidly removed the ropes from the wrists of the women and tied the hands of both his prisoners behind their backs. He then used a confiscated knife to slice their belts and strip both prisoners from the waist down.

Both traumatized women were wide-eyed and shaking like wind-blown maple leaves.

"Young man, what are you doing to these animals? It would give me great pleasure if you would just finish them off!"

"I'm just looking for electronics and weapons, ma'am. You see these wires here? They're attached to terminals embedded in his knees and ankles. Unless I pull them out, his bosses will know exactly where I've taken him. He must be the leader between these two. He's the one with all the wires."

He used a knife and began plucking at the wires, disconnecting them from the embedded terminals. "These guys are my prisoners. I'll interrogate them later. Maybe we can get some answers."

"We didn't think anyone would come for us," Betsy said. "We assumed you were all dead. Are there more survivors? What about Di, uh, that is, Diamond?"

"Di's alive and well. She'll be glad to see you."

"*Ha!* I doubt she really cares," Tige said. "She's only glad to see herself, mostly."

"Di insisted on comin' with me to rescue you. I had to fight her off to keep her from coming. Look in my back pocket. The pink shoes are hers. I watched her pull 'em right off her own feet so you wouldn't have to walk back barefoot. She reminded me to pick up a second pair so you'd both have shoes."

Cody's demeanor was all business. "I need to get these collars off your necks. These can be activated by someone at a central location. I've encountered it before. These prisoners may not be the only ones who can activate them."

Both women looked horrified.

"Don't worry, I'll be able to persuade them to cooperate."

The man with all the wires began to wake up. "What the . . . Uh, who are you?"

"I'm the new guy," Cody said. "You're my property now."

"*Hahaha!* And a comedian too. You won't get off this island. We'll find you no matter where you go. This won't end well for you. These women belong to us."

"I'm gonna ask you nicely for the combination to these collars," Cody said as he pulled the handgun from his belt.

"*Ha!* You won't pull that trigger here. It'll alert the company and this place will be swarming with more trouble than you've ever seen in your life."

Cody responded. "You're right. I dunno what I was thinking. I need a silencer." He stuck the muzzle into the left ear of the wired-up killer and pushed hard. "I have a silencer. If I pull this trigger right now, your brain will absorb ninety-six-point-eight-percent of the sound. And you won't hear very well afterwards."

"Now, wait a second. It'll do no such thing. Where'd you hear that?"

"Listen to me. I watched you kill a good man this afternoon in cold blood. I don't think you're ready to meet God right now, sir, but I can arrange the meeting if you don't gimme that combo. What's it gonna be?"

"It's in my back pocket."

"Now that's more like it." Cody retrieved the prisoner's dungarees and found the number. It worked. Both women breathed a sigh.

Cody placed the collars on the necks of the two prisoners. "These are yours now, gentlemen. I have the remote in my possession, so I can activate these collars whenever I please."

Cody motioned to the women. "Okay, ladies, I need you to carry their Radian 5 combat boots and their dungarees. The boots have a unique tread signature, too easy to track, so they're going back barefoot. I might have use for the boots later."

"*Yessir!*" Tige blurted, attempting to calm her vocal tremors.

Then she glared at the prisoners. "You guys are lucky. If I were runnin' this show, I'd slit your throats."

"I can't believe Di gave us her shoes," Betsy said. "I couldn't have gone another step without shoes. Look at my feet and you'll see why."

"Noted, ma'am. I couldn't help but notice. Will you be able to make it back to the beach?"

Betsy lowered her tone to impersonate his voice. "*Affirmative, Captain America!*"

They began walking back toward the shoreline, retracing their steps from earlier. Cody picked up the pouch he had left on the ground and deposited all the seized weapons and electronics into it. He now possessed guns, knives, and a remote for the collars. He had also taken military ops communication devices from both men. Thankfully, he had struck so quickly that the abductors had not been able to alert their bosses, whoever they were. Strangely, the men had been carrying no cellular phones.

It was a brisk march — Cody, his two prisoners wearing undies and no shoes, and two women with blond hair and sore feet. The ladies had asked Cody if they could wear the combat boots but Cody refused the request, saying, "They're too big for your feet and too heavy. You wouldn't be able to keep up and you'd end up with blisters. Besides, like I said, they're too easy to track. They leave a deep print. Takes longer to disappear."

When they came to the edge of the jungle, the beach lay before them. The euphoria of being suddenly free seemed to overtake the women. Cody had been expecting it.

Betsy was the first to react when she saw the beach. "What's your name, commander? Are you for real? I mean, have you ever thought about a career in motion pictures? Making movies?"

"Yeah," Tige agreed. "You have a nice face. I'd love to see you without your shirt sometime."

"Forget it," Betsy chided. "He's way too young for you, honey."

"Well, at least I'm not some Hollywood relic like you. By the way, Sir Galahad, we'd both like to know your name. Where'd you hear about using someone's brain for a silencer? That would make a great storyline."

Cody took a deep breath and shook his head wearily, but made no verbal response.

"So . . . would you really have pulled the trigger?" Betsy asked.

"We have a long way to go, ladies. The rest of the trip won't afford us much cover. We're exposed when we hit the beach. Besides that, look to the south. That's another storm brewing. It's gonna overtake us if we don't keep moving. How are your feet holding up?"

"South? Which way's south?" Tige asked. "Oh, there it is! We need to find shelter."

"You didn't answer my question. I asked about your feet."

"They're killing me," Tige told him. "Where can we find a cave to, uh, hunker down? That's how we'd do it in a blockbuster production."

"It's better if we pick up the pace and keep going, ladies. A good storm will provide cover from anyone tryin' to find us. They'll probably take shelter somewhere, so we'll have the advantage if we keep going. Besides that, if we can beat the storm to our hideout, the rain will wash out our tracks."

"I didn't think about that."

"So I ask again. Can you walk another mile?"

"Oh, oh, yes, of course."

"Fine with me," Betsy agreed. "Good idea, but can we just dip our feet in the water for a minute? Maybe it'll stop the burning."

"You have thirty seconds," Cody said.

The women left their shoes on the beach and waded into shallow water, looking toward the coming storm. The wind was eerily calm.

"I wasn't gonna pull the trigger," Cody said. "The human brain is not a silencer. Besides that, he wasn't ready—"

Tige interrupted. "I know, I know. He wasn't ready to, like, meet Jesus, or something like that, right?"

Cody nodded. "Plus, I need to interrogate them. These collars should help. We gotta find out what's goin' on."

"*Ha!* That punk must've believed your statistics about using the brain to silence a gunshot."

"Not for a second," Cody stated flatly. "But I made him believe that *I* thought it would work."

Tige playfully kicked up water with her foot. "Do you think he was bluffing about his buddies being near enough to hear the shot?"

Betsy interjected, "That doesn't matter now, sweetie. Our able commander had the better bluff. I can't believe you fell for it too, you little twit."

Tige ignored the insult. "What a *kickass* poker face! Is that your real face, or are you wearing a mask?" she snickered. "And what was that thing you slung the rock with?"

One of the prisoners finally spoke up. "He's just a kid, ladies. I dunno who he is. He wasn't supposed to be on that flight, but he will never leave this island, and neither will you."

Cody's face was stoic, his weary eyelids no indicator of emotion.

The other prisoner followed up. "You have no idea what you've stumbled onto, mate. We're just grunts, but the power behind us goes way higher than you can imagine. Billions in cash. With our technology, we'll soon be the only ones left standing. Who are you, anyway?"

"I can be your biggest nightmare, or your best ally."

"Don't make us laugh. A man of your skills should be smart enough to know who has the winning hand in the end."

"I'm here doing God's work. My Boss has no end, no beginning, and no equal. Your billions won't matter. Our battles are won by prayer warriors like my own mother who knows how to take hold of Heaven, not by technicians who worship money and cybertronics."

"Should that scare us? You're just a headcase, mate."

"You should be scared of the possibility that I *was* supposed to be on that plane after all."

"*Geesh!*" Betsy said. "You're like some . . . some medieval religious crusader rescuing damsels in distress, and then telling the bad guys to get ready to . . . to go to Hell or something. Not that I'm ungrateful, but . . . Oh, please . . . *your mother?*"

Tige couldn't resist. "How old are you anyway, crusader? Tell us your name. Are you channeling a younger Brad Pitt?"

"And what about that thing you used to sling that rock?" Betsy asked.

"It's called a shepherd's sling," Cody explained. "It's like the weapon David used to slay Goliath."

"But that story's a myth. So how did you manage to build this weapon based on legendary fiction?"

The first prisoner had more words for Cody. "It's been a long twenty-four hours for you, cowboy. You're sleepwalkin'. You won't even make it another mile."

Betsy stiffened her face. "You'd better hope nothin' happens to our crusader, because I'm staying next to him, and if he goes down, I'll get the remote outta his pocket and burn your heads off. Right now, he's the only one keeping you alive."

Just then, a clap of thunder rolled over the water like cannon fire. The wind picked up. Both women freaked.

Cody tossed them their shoes. "Time to go ladies. That storm will be here quicker than I thought."

~   ~   ~

Diamond waited on needles and pins for Cody's return from his foolish mission-impossible attempt to rescue Betsy and Tige. She fought her emotions all afternoon, trying to believe that Cody might actually be successful. Parker's confidence in him along with his description of Cody's survival training at the hands of former Navy SEALs had buoyed her hopes, but her mind kept telling her that her heart would not get what it wanted.

She tried to convince herself that it didn't matter, that it was none of her concern. Cody was, after all, just a kid with over-active testosterone out to prove his manhood, and Tige and Betsy were merely business associates who could be replaced, right?

But it mattered. It mattered as though her life depended on it. Why?

Victor and Parker spent their time gathering up more useful

items from the plane. Some were floating, some had already washed onto the beach. They also gathered driftwood and fallen branches to use for firewood. Nightfall was still several hours away, but a fire would be their only source of light inside the cave.

Diamond helped the two men retrieve items from the water and carry them up the hill. He feet began to hurt. She missed her shoes. Why had she given them away to two women who probably would not even return? Was it faith or stupidity?

Finally, she sat down near the entrance looking wistfully in the direction she had last seen Cody. It was getting late. She could see the ominous storm offshore — dark swirling clouds, lightning putting on a spectacular show. Should she pray that it would not reach land and catch Cody, Tige and Betsy out in the open? When the wind began to whistle up the hill and thunder shook the ground, she lost hope.

Suddenly the heavens opened up and cold rain with pea-sized hail forced her back inside. She maintained her watch from there, but was convinced that Cody and her two associates were never coming back. This day was ending badly. Things had gone from bad to worse. She glanced at her swollen, bleeding feet and began to sob. Parker noticed. He put his arm around her shoulders, but she shrugged away.

~   ~   ~

Cody pushed everyone, attempting to outrun the brewing storm. When they finally reached the last quarter mile, they were assaulted by ice pellets from the sky. Lightning struck a nearby tree, sending branches crashing to the ground. Adrenaline alone drove them the remaining quarter mile until at last they reached their destination.

"Our hideout's just up this hill. Follow me!" He looked up and saw someone haphazardly moving down the slope toward him.

"Cody!" The voice belonged to Diamond, bolting down the hill, slipping and sliding on her bare feet. "Victor! Mr. Parker! Get down here!" she screamed. "Cody's back!"

As Cody used his last ounces of strength to climb upward, Victor and Parker caught up with Diamond halfway down the slope and took the prisoners from Cody.

Cody faltered to one knee and began to slip as gravity, mud, and blinding rain rendered him helpless to stop his slide. Diamond blanked out momentarily, uncertain as to what she should do. She glanced up toward the cave and realized that Victor and Parker had their hands full with the prisoners. No one was coming to help Cody.

Instinctively, she grabbed him with both hands, but she was not strong enough to save him from his fall. They collapsed in each other's arms and rolled downward toward the bottom of the hill.

Unable to stop her emotions from spinning out of control, Diamond began kissing his face, making squealing noises and laughing while they helplessly slid in the mud and rain.

Tige and Betsy turned around and watched from the top of the hill.

"Is that *our* Di?" Tige asked. "Does she have any idea what kind of guy this Cody really is?"

"The kind of guy who always gets the girl, sweetie."

7

ME TOO

After rolling halfway down the hill in the pouring rain, Cody and Diamond lay in the muddy grass locked in an embrace that lasted several seconds.

The bug-eyed spectators at the top of the hill were surprised, but not as much as Cody and Diamond. They stared at each other in disbelief, their faces covered in grass and mud. Diamond had ended up on top of Cody.

She sat up, placed her hands on her face and gasped. Spontaneity was not part of her vocabulary. She had never had so much fun, yet had never hated herself more. Cody's reaction was just opposite.

"Cody! Why are you laughing?"

He regained control long enough for a short answer. "You're sitting on top of me!"

She rolled off into the mud. Suddenly, she felt the chill from the rain. "I don't know what happened." She held her rain-drenched hair out of her eyes. "I mean, I've never done anything like that before!" She shivered. *"Cody! What's so funny?"*

"I've never been tackled by a girl before!"

"I didn't tackle you. You tackled me!" She strained her hoarse vocal cords.

"And you kissed me again!" he hollered.

"Well, you kissed me back."

"I did not!" He laughed some more.

The couple looked up to realize they were now surrounded by the snickering faces of Parker, Tige, and Betsy who had come to help. Just then a thunder clap shook the ground. They all jumped out of their skins, which unlocked the pent-up hilarity that Diamond had tried desperately to keep under wraps. She helplessly doubled over with her own round of laughter, prompting everyone else to follow.

As the group moved up the hill, Cody was barely able to walk. When they entered the lava cave, he collapsed on the floor soaking wet and shivering.

"Don't say a word!" Diamond barked at her two associates who were likewise suffering from cold and fatigue, but who could not resist staring and snickering as they sat next to a warm fire.

The sun had not yet settled below the horizon, but the heavy squalls had brought on early darkness.

Cody's arms and face were cold, his hands shaking. He was depleted after the long night of searching for crash survivors followed by a day filled with murder, rescuing two women, and running from the storm.

Despite her embarrassment and anger at herself for losing control in front of everyone, Diamond now understood that Cody was the only one who could lead them. Their survival would rest upon his skills. She couldn't let anything happen to him.

She handed Cody an energy bar. "We found these in one of the bags today," she told him. "We have enough to last us two days if each of us eats just one per day." She tore open the wrapper. "Eat. That's an order."

He struggled to his feet and crammed the bar into his mouth

and spoke while he chewed. "What's that flickering?"

She handed him a cup of rainwater. "Mr. Parker starting a fire. He and Victor gathered dry wood today so we could have a fire tonight." She rubbed his face and tried to warm his skin. "Cody, you're freezing. Would you let someone help you out of these wet clothes?"

He took a long look into her eyes and softened his hard face. "I'm done in."

"Oh? As if I couldn't figure that out for myself?"

He ran his hand through Diamond's dripping-wet hair. "I'd say you're not exactly dripping with dryness yourself."

"Cody, that made no sense. Dripping with dryness?"

He leaned toward her and collapsed upon her. He was heavy. She turned for help and realized that everyone had been watching. Tige and Betsy stepped up, immediately taking hold of his shoulders. They helped Diamond ease his sleeping body onto a spot they had prepared on the floor.

Diamond looked at her two friends and tried not to imagine what they might have endured. Crusher had been murdered while they had stood just inches away from him. They had been forced to wear electro-shock collars. She could see dark bruises and red burns in the shape of the collar on each of their necks.

Diamond was suddenly overwhelmed by uncontrollable grief. Hot tears welled in her eyes while she held out her arms to her two friends. All three women joined in a tearful embrace.

"Di, you have cuts and bruises all over your feet," Betsy said. "We couldn't believe you would sacrifice your shoes for us."

"We take each other for granted," Di said. "And it's especially me that's guilty. I never knew how much I cared for you both until I thought I had lost you."

"What about this hulk lyin' on the ground behind you?" Tige's eyes lit up. "So his name's Cody? What's his last name? What does he do, anyway?"

"Listen, he's twenty-two and he's highly-trained."

Betsy reacted with flair. "*Oooh*, we hadn't noticed! I mean, Dibird, you should've seen this guy!" She leaned over, still trying to gain back her strength from the long run in the storm.

"That's right," Tige said, still breathing heavily. "He's better than the stunt guys we film. Maybe you can talk him into letting me represent him."

"Tiger, I don't think he wants to make movies," Di said. "He's too busy doing God's work."

Tige threw her hands up. "Well, why didn't you just say that earlier?"

Betsy piled it on. "Look, I love this guy, but . . . I mean, his *mother* prays for him, so he says, like that's the secret of his strength, or something."

Diamond responded out of character. "I wish my mother had prayed for me."

"So . . . Di, this is not you. You can't say things like that. What about your fans? What about the magazines and tabloids?"

"Listen," Diamond said. "The two of you need to get out of those wet clothes, but first things first. We need Cody. We may not survive without him. He needs to shed his wet clothes too, but he's out for the count. Parker and Victor are busy securing the prisoners in a hole we discovered today in the back. So it's up to us. I need the two of you to help me while Cody's asleep."

"What? You want us to strip his clothes off?"

Diamond explained. "Look, today we found thirty comfort blankets floating in the water. The airline carried them in individual water-tight wrapping in the overhead compartments. We can just put a couple of blankets over Cody, then reach underneath and get his clothes. Piece of cake."

Betsy crossed her arms. "Listen, Sweet Ebony, this guy eats nails instead of Wheaties. He makes fools out of psychos who like to shoot people In broad daylight. I don't wanna mess with him."

Diamond softened her volume but sharpened her tongue. "On the other hand, ladies, he has a mother who prays for him. He doesn't hurt women."

Tige's eager eyes beamed. "I'll do it. Don't worry about using any blankets. He's not gonna wake up."

"You keep your hands off him!" Diamond stiffened up.

Tige lost her grin. "What's the matter with you, Di? He's dead to the world. Just look at him. He'll never know."

"Something known as respect." Diamond picked up two blankets. "Here, just hold these blankets over him and I'll get his clothes. We can't afford for him to get pneumonia. He's our best hope, or have you not noticed?"

The storm along the shoreline continued to rage until late into the night. Fortunately, Victor and Joe had gone hunting for dry firewood in and around the cave earlier. Joe had found several friction-fired lighters in the carry-on luggage. Hence, the cave was comfortably lighted by a flickering fire.

This was the first night the survivors had spent together. The evening before, everyone had been disoriented after the crash. Some had slept all night where they had collapsed on the beach and had awakened unable to remember what had happened. Now, everyone remembered, and the ugly memories began to take hold.

Cody slept soundly next to the fire which provided their only light. Caribbean air was warm at night, but the falling rain was cold, having originated from high-altitude thunderclouds, thus cooling the ambient night air.

Diamond placed his wet clothes and hers on the rock ledge to dry near the fire. She made certain the blankets were secure around Cody. She wrapped herself in a similar manner and sat next to him, but she remained awake until midnight when the rain finally stopped.

Victor and Joe had decided to sleep near the prisoners for security reasons. The two perpetrators would be interrogated the next morning.

A few minutes after midnight, Diamond finally drifted off to sleep. An hour later, her dreams startled her. Images of the crash — the nearness of the waves as seen through the windshield before they splashed down and the crying of passengers, many of whom were now dead — dreams as vivid as the moments each happened. She was suddenly awake and wide-eyed.

She stared at Cody's face, still smudged but softly illuminated by the crackling fire. He looked at peace, but she knew that he must be dreaming too. What were his thoughts? At that moment, Cody awakened and found her eyes. "Me too," he said. Then he drifted off again. She shook her head and rubbed her eyes. Did that really happen? Had she imagined it?

She could faintly hear her two friends sobbing, comparing their recollections about the events surrounding the crash. They also talked about what had happened after they were captured. She could not hear the details, but she knew they were greatly traumatized.

She decided not to join them. Cody and Victor would debrief them in the morning, and that would certainly be enough pain for her friends to endure.

Should she talk to God? Even if He existed, why would He listen to her? Parker had told her earlier to make a commitment of her life to Jesus, but that was too much to ask. She wasn't the benevolent, loving person that Parker thought she was, and her unachieved goals were more important.

She was part African American, had no siblings, and was estranged from her parents, but she had kept other details about her childhood secret. She wanted to be more than just a star. Diamond wanted to be the voice of America, the country whose image as the land of opportunity had faded. She must please her producers, and most of all, herself.

She closed her eyes wondering what tomorrow would bring. They were living in an information void. What island was this? Who was responsible for bringing them here? Would they ever get rescued? Who was Joe Parker? He obviously knew more than he was telling, and he seemed the least surprised of anyone by the events which had transpired.

Why was she so captivated by Cody? She had met the hottest men in Hollywood — men who could dazzle any woman. But, strangely, it wasn't Cody's physical attributes that attracted her. It was something deeper. She was undone in his presence, and yet she felt more whole than ever in her life. How could that happen in just thirty six hours?

She almost resented him for it. She had thought that becoming a screen star would change the lifelong image she carried about herself. But even now, she was still that person she had hated for as long as she could remember. Cody had an iron jaw and steel fists, and a mother who prayed for him. There was compassion in his soul that her friends could not see. What could possibly have made him that way?

How did he feel about rolling in the mud with her? The kiss? He certainly did not seem as troubled by it as she. Hopefully, he would not remember it in the morning.

She lay down beside him wrapped in her own blanket, hoping that upon his waking he would not feel she had encroached upon his space. After all, she had stripped him of his clothing while he was sleeping, and had stood guard over him like a nesting swallow. *Oh, God, if you're really there . . .*

She finally drifted into another restless sleep.

~   ~   ~

Daylight arrived none too soon for Diamond. The thunderous storms of last night were gone. She arose quietly and tiptoed around Cody to get to her clothes which she had placed near the fire next to his. They were almost dry. She strolled to the back end of the cave where she and Parker had discovered a waterfall the previous day.

They had also found a back exit from the cave just large enough for an average adult to squeeze through. In between this new opening and the waterfall, they had found the hole which was now serving as a holding cell for the prisoners.

Diamond noticed that Victor was sitting atop the hole, keeping an eye on the two killers Cody had captured. He and Parker had taken turns watching them during the night. Victor was holding a weapon.

"Morning, Vic. I see you're wide awake. I wanna step around the corner and stand under the waterfall a few minutes, okay?"

Victor waved back but looked half asleep.

She walked around the bend to the falls, dropped her blanket and clothes to the floor, then stood under the cool water for a minute. It wasn't hot, but it was wet. The water that fell from the ceiling was crystal clear and flowed into a reservoir that ran about twenty feet until apparently seeping through to another cave at the next level below them.

When she finished, she picked up one of the coffee mugs they had salvaged from the floating luggage and filled it with water. They had left several mugs sitting there for anyone who wanted to drink. She downed a few swallows of the cool, clear water and got dressed.

When she approached the section where she had left Cody sleeping near the fire, she heard Tige and Betsy snickering. They were up to something. She quickened her steps when she heard Cody speaking.

"The show's over, ladies. You wanna tell me who stole my clothes?"

"I'll never tell," Tige's devilish voice shrilled out.

When Diamond entered the scene, Cody's accusatory look and heavy scowl were tempered by a wry grin of his own. It was obvious that he knew exactly who the thief was. Diamond stopped in her tracks as though *she* were the one standing there without a shirt.

"Uh-oh," Betsy said. "Too bad we aren't filming."

Cody was wearing his dungaree britches, but he was holding his shirt. This was the first time he had looked human in two days. He wasn't exactly Mr. Universe. His upper body was ripped but average, and his arms did not appear capable of such fury as they did most certainly possess.

Cody walked toward her and placed his hands on her shoulders. "I knew you were there during the night, even though I was, like, totally zoned out. Thanks for keeping me warm."

"Keeping you warm?" She turned and frowned at her two giggling associates.

Cody grinned innocently. "Any idea where my skivvies went?"

Diamond's mouth flew open. "What?" She looked down, then quickly back up. "You mean—?"

Tige sniggled. *"Skivvies?* What's that?"

Diamond marched over and held out her hand. "You give me those or you're fired!"

Tige immediately produced them. Diamond jerked Cody's boxers back from her and handed them to Cody, saying, "When I left to take a shower, there were three adults sleeping in this room, but now all I can see are three adolescents."

Cody picked up a blanket. "Even an adolescent needs a shower once in a while. I'll just follow the falling-water sound 'til I find it."

Diamond offered to lead the way, which elicited whooping and whistling sounds from her two mischievous friends.

"You've done enough," Cody said. "I can find it myself."

~   ~   ~

When Cody returned from his shower, Diamond and her friends were talking quietly. "I don't want to interrupt," Cody said. "We have a busy day. Gotta find some answers. First, I need to talk to you two ladies. Can we do that?"

Tige's face answered clearly enough — she was not on board.

Betsy fidgeted. "Sweetie, Cody needs to debrief us about what happened."

"I'd like for Victor to join us," Cody said. "If that's okay."

Tige hid her face. "I can't talk about it. I just need to forget and leave this friggin' place. I wanna go home."

Cody pulled up a log that Victor had brought into the cave the day before. He sat down.

"You know, Tige, you're stronger than you think."

"With all respect, Cody, you don't know anything about me."

"I know all I need for now. Something horrible has happened to you, but I can see you have enough saltiness and humor in you to be a survivor."

Tige made a confession. "I watched you wake up . . . when you came outta the blanket," she mused. "I mean, I couldn't help myself, and you just laughed it off and didn't even get mad."

Diamond weighed in. "Cody, this morning we saw a glimpse of the human in you. I mean, there's nothing wrong with acting adolescent once in a while."

Tige couldn't resist. "You mean like rollin' in the mud? Like yesterday?"

Cody stared innocently. "Mud? I'm not sure what you're talkin' about."

The giggling from Tige and Betsy was shortlived as Diamond glared at them.

Tige frowned. "I still don't know if I can . . . I mean I don't wanna discuss what happened to us. Not ever."

Cody forced a grin. "Okay, I will admit that I don't smile much. When I laugh, people are shocked. Most of my work is under the radar, secrets I can't talk about, so I hold it inside. Maybe I need a little more humor in my life too."

Diamond sat down beside Cody and placed her hand on his knee. When Cody's knee started to twitch, she withdrew.

Cody leaned forward. "Sometimes, the best thing you can do is tell someone, talk to somebody who understands. So . . . maybe I should go first. You wanna hear how my week has gone so far?"

Cody had their undivided attention. "Two days ago in a Caracas back-street alley I stumbled upon a newborn in a dumpster. He was a screamer, a survivor, a kindred spirit sounding off a loud SOS."

Tige covered her lips with a shaking right hand.

"I was late for a meeting with my contact. The lives of hundreds depended on it. But this one child . . . I had to decide whether to make the rendezvous or save this kid. Someone had just thrown him away like a . . . like a piece o' garbage." He ran his hands through his hair. His knee began to fidget like before.

Diamond leaned easily against him and rested her hand on his knee again. This time, it stopped bouncing.

"Somehow . . . I knew I was destined to save that little boy. After I dug him out of the garbage, I was chased by five hostiles. I ran down the alley and turned . . ."

He paused with distant eyes, replaying the event in his mind.

Diamond was afraid he wouldn't finish. She held her breath and squeezed his hand. "What happened next, Cody?"

"I was on foot, running out of options. All-a-sudden, I see this crowd. This lady, she says somethin' like, 'Sir, we have your coat and hat ready.'"

Diamond leaned closer. "Was she your contact?"

"No. I've never seen her before. So, she puts this bright-striped coat and huge sombrero on me and lets me wear them until the bad guys pass on by. Then, the same lady says something like, 'The little treasure you're holding under your shirt will arrive safely, so don't worry.'"

Betsy spoke up. "Cody, what happened to that newborn?"

"I ended up at an old boarding house where a man and wife help battered teenage girls get out of the country. A fifteen-year-old girl had just lost her own baby. She had 'bout given up on life 'til she saw this kid I brought in. She accepted him as a gift from God. Now, the little loudmouth has a mom to care for him, and the mom . . . well, she has a son."

The story made huge tears roll down Tige's cheeks. "*Ohhh,*" she whispered. "That was beautiful."

Diamond's ebony eyes misted. "Oh, Cody. I had no idea."

"So, two hours later, I'm on this plane that falls out of the sky, and here we are. Now, you know why my mother prays for me."

Betsy shook her head. "I always thought guys like you — I mean, butt-hard military types — were just all about bringing rough justice, hurting people. I need a break. I'll be back in a few."

When Betsy left, Cody stayed seated. He hung his head in his hands and sighed wearily. Diamond could see the obvious — he was too exhausted to move. She expected Tige to follow Betsy out, but Tige remained seated across from Cody with her hand over her eyes. Diamond had never seen her hardnosed associate display emotion other than anger or devious laughter, but Cody's story about the child in the dumpster had obviously stirred something in her.

Diamond stood up. "I'll go get you some water and another power bar, Cody. I mean . . . you look zonked."

Tige glanced up and made eye contact with Diamond while attempting to hold back tears. Diamond nodded and departed, leaving her alone with Cody.

Diamond stood to her feet. "I'm gonna get you another power bar and some water, Cody. I mean . . . you look zonked."

Tige raised her head slightly and made eye contact with Diamond while attempting to hide tears. Di nodded back and left her alone with Cody.

Cody watched Diamond disappear, then spoke to Tige.

"You're pretty good at the game, aren't you," Cody concluded.

Tige looked up. "Game?"

"Stealing skivvies and wearing a party face can only take you so far when it really hurts," Cody said.

"What gave me away?" She chuckled through dry lips. "You don't miss much." She swallowed hard. "Why do you even care?"

He looked into her face with an amiable smile but said nothing.

She pulled her eyes away. "You don't fool me for a minute."

"You don't fool me, either, Tige. You are a strong woman, but we're only fooling ourselves if we believe our strength is always sufficient."

She straightened her face and stared through unbelieving eyes. "Let me guess; the god thing, right?" She waited, then softened her tone. "So you must hate me. You think I'm going to Hell or something."

He shook his head. "Look, if there's a God who really sees, really hears, really loves you, wouldn't you wanna know Him?"

"Well, who wouldn't want to know a god like that? Too bad he or it doesn't exist." She waited, but he said nothing.

"So, crusader, aren't you gonna argue with me?"

Cody never took his eyes off her, but did not respond.

"Look, Cody. I've . . . I've disrespected you. I shouldn't have swiped your skivs. I can see you're a good guy. I mean, you didn't even get mad. I almost hoped you would. Don't you ever crack?"

Cody ran his fingers through his coarse hair. "Can you keep a secret?" He sighed heavily. "I'm not as experienced as everybody thinks. I mean, I've been on some missions, but nothing of this magnitude, and I've never been in charge. I didn't appoint myself the leader here. I stumbled into it. Victor's a good man, but he's injured and limping. Besides that, his eyes tell me he's more used to following orders than giving them. He depends on me, like everyone else."

Tige frowned. "So, why are you telling me this?"

"Why? So you'll know I'm feeling my way along just like you are. I have more defensive skills than most, but I'm scared too."

"Scared? You? So . . . what do you fear the most, if I may ask?"

"I fear that I won't be able to protect everyone and get us all home. In our current situation, my own skills and strength aren't enough."

"You're afraid for us? But what about death? Isn't that your greatest fear? Wait. Let me guess. You don't fear dying, right?"

His ragged smile seemed hard-earned, laborious. "I've known plenty of wealthy people who say life has no purpose. A person may have everything to live for, but life seems meaningless when one has nothing to die for."

Tige's troubled eyes teared up again.

"We face impossible odds here," Cody told her. "But I decided to trust God when I was eight, and I trust Him now. I'm secure in that, living or dying. It will take a miracle to get us off this island in one piece, so if we do get home, you'll know exactly why."

8

DEE MCARTHUR SIMON

Cody remained alone for a few minutes after he and Tige broke up their powwow. Tige's reticence to further discuss matters of faith was no surprise. But she had been moved, and Cody wondered if he had handled the conversation wisely. Commanding a mission against hostiles was not his only area of inexperience.

Telling the heart-wrenching story about the infant had not been on his 'want to do' list, but it seemed situation-appropriate. He wondered if it would make it easier for the two women to tell about their traumatic hours of captivity.

Diamond returned with another energy bar and a mug of cool water.

"Here," she said to Cody. "Eat and drink."

He stuffed the energy bar into his mouth like before. "Good thing you found these. If we don't find a food source on this island, we're gonna be really hungry in a few days."

"What about fish or crab, or coconuts maybe?"

Just then Victor, Betsy, and Tige returned and sat down on the floor.

"We decided to invite Victor into the discussion after all," Tige said. "I want to do my part even if it's difficult. I wanna help us all go back to our lives."

Cody sat down on the log again. "Good. So, let's take it from the beginning."

Betsy started the dialogue. "They found us wandering on the beach at dawn the morning after the crash. We didn't even know where the crash site was."

"That's right," Tige said. "We had walked beyond the bend during the night. That's where they found us when the sun came up."

"First, they asked us if there were more survivors," Betsy said. "We didn't know anything, but they didn't believe us. That's the first time we saw those shock collars they were carrying in their backpacks."

"Yeah," Tige said. "They made us wear them and flipped the switch just to show they were serious. Then they —" Tige began to cough, gasping for breath, holding her throat.

Diamond and Betsy froze, but Cody reached out and took hold of Tige's shoulders. "Tige! Tige, can you hear me? Just breathe. They can't hurt you anymore. You're with friends now."

Her gray eyes stared into space, her hands clamped tightly around her throat. When Betsy and Diamond rallied around her, she gradually came out of it.

"I can't. I can't do this. I'm sorry."

Cody acceded. "No need to apologize. My bad. I should have let Victor take the lead on this. He has some specific questions. Answer only what you're comfortable with."

Victor spoke up. "Ladies, we need information about their activities — who you saw, what you observed, anything that might give us a clue as to who these characters are and why they brought us here. Did you see their center of operations?"

"No," Betsy said. "They wanted us to lead them to the crash site, but we took them the wrong direction at first. We finally turned around and came back this way."

"That's when . . . that's when we came upon the wreckage and the bodies," Tige said.

"I got the feeling they already knew where the crash site was," Betsy followed up. "They just wanted to see how long it would take us to figure it out. After they realized we didn't know anything, they . . . they shot Crusher and took us as prisoners."

"They were taking us to their headquarters when Cody caught up with us." Tige got up and paced across the floor.

Cody asked another question. "Did you hear anything about children? Before Crusher died, he told me about kids used as slave laborers."

Betsy looked at Tige inquisitively. Both shook their heads. "We don't remember anything about that."

"But they did say something about using us . . ." Tige's eyes grew larger than beach balls. "Something about genetic experiments, outer space travel, or . . ."

"Now it's coming back to me," Betsy said. "I remember a room with these amber lights." She caught her breath. "Children! Yes, I saw them."

Victor spoke again. "So, maybe they took you to their operation after all. Maybe it's just hard to remember."

Cody and Victor decided the women had been through enough. The rest could wait.

"We need to find food," Cody said. "It would be nice to just walk down and catch a fish or something like that, but if we leave this hideout we might be spotted."

"Well, gentlemen," Diamond spoke up, "if we sit in this cave too long, we'll starve. I say we take a chance."

Cody nodded. "For all it's worth, the bad guys may already know about this cave anyway. There's only one way to find out."

Diamond frowned. "Interrogation of the prisoners, right? Seems like these guys are master deceivers. How do you know if they're lying?"

I'll know," Victor said. "Besides, I'm not sure how masterful they are, the way they fell for Cody's brain gun-silencer stunt."

Tige blurted out. "*Ohhh*, you would've fallen for it too. Those guys were about to . . . I mean Cody even had me believin' he was gonna pull that trigger if the guy didn't give us the code for those collars."

"Alright, Vic, take a crack at the prisoners," Cody suggested. "But wait 'til this afternoon when they get real thirsty and hungry."

~   ~   ~

Following their morning meeting, Cody asked Diamond to show him the back exit from the cave. They walked past the area where the prisoners were held in a hole too deep for them to escape, then went around the corner to the shower area and came to a narrow adjoining tunnel which resembled the inside of a hollow pretzel made of smooth rock.

It was a smaller version of the lava tube they were using as living quarters, with walls that resembled layers and layers of smooth spun silk. After the first turn, they could see the light coming from somewhere ahead. They stepped along carefully, not knowing if reptiles might have already claimed the narrow subterranean grotto as their territory.

When they made their last turn, the exit was in full view. It was a smaller crawl-through tunnel about five feet in length with a jagged opening at the other end where an external force such as a falling boulder had smashed and broken down the tube, letting the sunlight come through. They crawled to the end and surveyed the outside terrain before exiting. The hole opened onto a downslope, and they could see in the distance a crater at least four hundred feet deep and a mile wide.

"Cody, this is breathtaking. I've never seen such majesty."

"So, do we dare stick our heads outside?"

"Oh, I must!" She began pulling herself through the opening.

"Wait!" Cody caught her arm. "Lemme check it out first." He pulled a set of field glasses out of his side pocket. Victor had found them washed up on the beach the day before.

He scanned the entire perimeter of the crater. "I see no sign of life." He became perfectly still. "Listen." He waited. "Do you hear that?"

"Hear what?"

"A faint hum. Hear it?"

"No, I don't hear anything," she whispered. "Wait. Yes, I do hear it. What does it mean?"

"Unknown, ma'am. Could be a submarine or other ocean-going vessel in Caribbean waters. Could just be the earth making its own vibrations."

Diamond snickered. "*Unknown, ma'am?* Cody, this is me you're talking to."

"Oh, yeah. You're the chick who recovered my skivvies. How could I forget?"

Cody climbed through the opening and took another look around. He spotted a secluded natural rock formation about five meters away.

"C'mon, there's a place we can talk over there." He helped her through the opening.

"Oh, you want to chat with me? In private? This could get interesting."

They sat on the ground facing each other. After an awkward moment, Cody broke the silence. "Your feet."

"Excuse me?" She looked down and wiggled her toes. "Very observant. What about my feet?"

"Bruised. Scratched."

"I'm letting Betsy wear my shoes for now. Her feet are worse than mine, and I'm tougher than you think."

"*Ha!* I know how tough you are. You fought me hard when I pulled you outta that plane."

"I fought you? I don't remember." She swallowed hard. "So then . . . why did you even bother?"

"Would you rather I had left you there?"

She lost her smuggish grin and looked downward pensively. "Well . . . I . . . I just wonder if — Uh, Cody, this ground we're sitting on; it feels like it's vibrating."

He put his hand on the ground. "I feel it . . . Now it's stopped. Could've been an earth tremor."

"What is this place? Another country? An island?"

Cody took a deep breath. "I watched the headings, course changes, airspeed. I timed each leg of the flight. We're in the middle of the Caribbean Sea, 'bout three hundred miles northeast of Caracas and three hundred west of Saint Vincent. We're in the middle of nowhere."

Diamond's voice trembled. "So, does this place have a name?"

He sighed. "No telling. Lots of undeveloped islands in this ocean. But somebody's using this as a base, and they're doing some really bad things."

"Oh, you think? Shootings, abducting people, hijacking commercial aircraft. Cody, how do we get out of here?"

"I'm thinking about sniffing out their base. Payin' them a visit. We need answers if we're gonna get off this island."

"Why do you have to be such a hero? Pay them a visit? Do you have a death wish?" She shook her head. "I know it's necessary. But I've never been strong. I've never been so scared."

"If you try to be strong on your own, you'll never make it. Everybody needs someone . . . I mean, like family, friends. *Together* we're strong, to use a cliché."

"What about you, Cody? Do you have anyone special who helps you be strong?"

"I have a close-knit family but I usually work alone. I've never had a girlfriend, if that's what you're asking. Right now my life's about other things. If I ever marry, I pray for someone who'll love me the way my mom loves my dad."

"My family is a cruel joke. My real name is Dee McArthur Simon. My mother is white. She's from Chicago. Her parents never forgave her for marrying a black man, and they never forgave me for just being born."

"Yikes. Not a good start."

"Well, it gets worse. When I was eleven, my father . . . my father started abusing me. I might as well say it; he raped me." She pounded her fist. "He came into my bedroom several nights a week."

She paused, trembling from head to toe. "So . . . so in addition to everything else, are you a therapist too? I mean, why am I even telling you this?"

"If you wanna stop . . . well, it's your call. I'm not a shrink or trained counselor. But I'm a good listener."

She hesitated for a minute, mesmerized by his deep blue eyes that seemed to ripen with passion. She pulled her knees up to her chest and surrounded them with her arms.

"When I was fourteen, my father started bringing his brother and some of his friends. They all . . . I mean, they all talked about my beauty, tried to make me feel pretty. I told my mother what they were doing to me, but she didn't believe me, or so she said. Then later, she changed her tune and told me I should be kind to my father because he had needs."

Diamond's lashes began to blink with heavy tears, but she was determined to continue. "I decided it was too dangerous to be beautiful, so I tried to make myself ugly. I figured they would leave me alone if I was ugly.

"So I stopped wearing makeup. I never showered. I started eating everything in sight. I was five-foot-six at age fifteen, and I soon weighed 265 pounds."

"*You?* You weighed 265?"

She closed her eyes. "Give me a minute. I'm not going to cry hysterically or choke. Just give me a second, okay?"

"Of course." Cody offered a reserved smile. "You're one of the most beautiful women I've ever seen. So what happened after that?"

She chuckled even as she wiped warm tears from her face. "Thank you, Cody. No man before has ever told me I was beautiful and really meant it."

He shifted his eyes downward.

"I found out my father had been charging the other men. I mean, he was renting me out. He was furious because I was *ruining his business!*"

She buried her face in her hands, yet she could not stop talking. "My parents locked me in my room and told me I could not eat until I had lost fifty pounds. I didn't think I could be humiliated any worse, but I was wrong."

Suddenly, Diamond fought the urge to get up and run as far away as she could. From Cody. From her life. From this island. But she was unable to pull herself away from him. Cody never raised his eyes.

"My uncle, one of my dad's best customers, was the preacher at Greater Ebenezer Church of Jesus, or something like that. So, that was my impression of Jesus."

Diamond paused to bring her trembling breath under control. "Eventually, Child Protective Services took me out of the home. I hated being beautiful, but I also hated what I had become. No one wanted to adopt me. Ironically, I stayed in school long enough to respond to a drama department invitation. *Ha!* They were doing a play called 'When the Fat Lady Sings.' Guess who got the leading part."

"Bravo!" Cody said. "I bet you were a *big* hit?"

"*Big* hit?" She began to laugh and couldn't stop. She let go of her knees and gave him a fake karate kick in the gut. "I'll have you know I received the actress of the year award at my school."

"Congratulations."

"Right then, I knew exactly how to get back at my parents and how to get even with God. I would become a professional actress and show everyone I was worth something after all. No one would ever mistreat me again."

"So, you changed your name and got on a fitness program and won the lead role in *Deep Water Crossing?*"

"That film made me a star, but . . . you didn't happen to see it, did you?"

Cody bit his lip. "No, I didn't see it, but I heard."

"So you know that taking off my clothes on camera made me famous. I'm so glad you didn't watch it, Cody."

"How did it make you feel?"

"While filming, I was humiliated. All of it came back — every single painful memory. But I was so *desperate* to succeed. When I won the Oscar, I was exhilarated. I was proud that I had made myself beautiful again. I called my father. I thought he would be proud of me. The only thing he said was, 'Dee, you ain't nothin.' And nothin's all you'll ever be.'"

She winced her eyes shut bitterly, as if to smother the haunting memory.

"I was rejected for the lead role of Daphne in *Moonlight at Camp David* because director Jesse Franks cited I was part Caucasian. He said it would be inappropriate for me to portray such an important African American woman."

Cody looked confused. "I'm part African American too. Why would anyone say that? Especially a prominent black director like Franks?"

"After that, I figured I didn't belong anywhere, black or white, and maybe my father was right."

"You've managed to become a megastar. So maybe your father was wrong after all."

"But I'm just kidding myself. I did only one nude scene, but it branded me. I started reading deeper into the comments of film critics. I'm popular only because of my 'physical assets', as they say. No one wants me for my skills. I'm only an object to be used by strangers, just like when I was in my father's house."

Cody treaded softly. "So, other than the fact I'm a good listener, why are you telling me this?"

"Have I made myself a fool in front of you?"

"Well," he smiled tentatively. "After the way we rolled down the hill together in the mud, we aren't exactly strangers."

"I had hoped you wouldn't remember. I still cannot believe what I did."

"Yeah, we were both a little wacko yesterday."

Her face clouded. "It's this . . . this island, the uncertainty, crazy emotions. I've never wanted to tell anyone my story. I wanted to forget. My handlers say I shouldn't reveal that I'm a victim, because it makes me look weak. Bad Karma, bad for my career, they say. But I may be dead tomorrow. All of a sudden, I have to face myself."

She brushed the hair from her eyes. "I don't blame people for not loving me. No one ever has. I don't even love myself. I drive people away. Maybe that's what happens when your whole life's just an act. Nothing about me is real."

"I can't pretend to know what you've been through," Cody said. "I've never been abused. But welcome to the world of being real. You just made your first step."

They were silent for a moment. The sun was nearly overhead by now, and they sat in the shade beneath a clump of palms that seemed to be growing right out of the rocks. The air was still.

"Di, I'm sorry you have such a low opinion of Jesus. Have you ever heard the word *agape*?"

"I'm confused. What?"

"So, it's a word with roots in the Holy Land. See, Jesus told His followers to do the impossible. Like . . . like forgive people who hurt you, like reach out to suffering individuals, even people who hate you. But, we aren't capable of doin' that on our own."

"Forgive people who've hurt me? Why should I do that?"

"Well, see, Jesus has a style of His own. He's in a class by Himself. He made a promise to anyone seriously wanting a new life that He'd fill them with his own eternal Spirit if they would lay down their lives for Him."

"What does that mean? I have to die?"

"It means you give the ownership of your life to Him. Give up a life you're gonna lose anyway, and gain a life that nothing can take from you. His Spirit seals the deal, living inside you with a love so consuming it lets you hear God in your heart."

"Okay, that almost sounds spooky. So what does this *agape* word have to do with it?"

"The first Jesus followers had no adequate word in Greek or Hebrew to describe this new life, so . . . they sorta modified an older Greek word that meant friendship, and came up with the word agape. It means a love way beyond friendship. It's so strong you can *invade* the impossible, as my mom likes to say."

"Impossible?" She tilted her head. "You mean, love that can make you risk your life for a child in a garbage bin?" She couldn't take her eyes off his. "And the woman with the hat and coat who somehow expected you?"

He nodded slowly.

Just then, thunder rumbled and echoed through the hills.

"Cody, it's gonna rain. We should get back in the cave. But first, Mr. Parker told me about praying. I told him I didn't know how. Do you think if we pray, God might provide food for everyone? I mean, maybe if I just listen to you, I can learn how. Not that I'm, as you say, committed, like a real Christian or anything. But Cody, if what you just said is true . . . I mean, it sounds too good to be true. Most things that sound that way, well, sadly enough, they usually are not true. But, I mean —"

He cut her off and blurted, "God in Heaven, I'm callin' on You right now, here with this beautiful soul sitting next to me."

He clasped both her hands in his. She awkwardly bowed her head.

"We're askin' You to provide food for us all, Lord. And please consider doing it in a hurry. A beached shark closer to us, or maybe you could send an Angel to, like, drop something off. We appreciate it, Lord. Okay, well, Amen."

They stared at each other. "I'm not really too good at prayin' out loud either," he said apologetically. "I just tell God what I'm feelin' at the time. I mean, He knows anyway, so I don't use a lotta clever, fancy words."

"Cody, we need to get inside. I just felt a raindrop."

They moved back toward the cave opening and stopped in their tracks.

"Cody! What's that . . . that thing sitting right there? It's a backpack! I don't recognize it. Somebody's been here!"

"Hurry! Get inside. I'll check it out. Could be a bomb." He looked in every direction. "How did somebody leave this here without us seein' them?"

She moved toward the opening then looked back. "You're not gonna open that thing, are you?"

He motioned her to keep going. She scrambled inside, but could not refuse the temptation to watch him through the aperture.

He knelt down. The camouflage army backpack looked innocent enough, but was it safe? It did not belong to anyone among the survivors, and he didn't recognize it. He placed his ear close to the object and listened. He clearly heard an old-style alarm clock ticking. Diamond knew something was wrong when Cody's face turned as white as a snow ghost.

"It's a ticking bomb!" he shouted, backing away. "Get away from the entrance!" Suddenly the alarm sounded. He hit the ground and covered his head with his hands.

Nothing happened.

"Cody? Why are you lying there like that?"

He crawled over to the backpack and carefully opened it up. He pulled out the clock, stared a moment, then laughed so hard Diamond thought he would never stop. Finally, Cody lay on his back with raindrops falling on his face and raised his hands as though he would hug the overhead cloud.

9

GOLD

Cody lay on the ground near the back entrance of the cave. He reached heavenward as raindrops pelted his face. A lightning bolt flashed before his eyes, bringing him back to reality. Then, he saw a beautiful figure with raven hair and deep eyes standing over him. She appeared upside down.

"Cody! Get up! It's pouring. I'll have to hang your clothes by the fire again."

Cody jumped up. "C'mon, let's get inside." He grabbed the backpack, threw the alarm clock inside and pulled her toward the cave. They climbed through the opening.

"What's in the pack? Let me see it!" She jerked it away. When she looked inside, she stared with mouth wide open.

Finally, she squeaked out, "I can't believe it! Cody, I can't believe it!"

Cody reached in, pulled out the clock, and showed her the face of it.

"From Angel? Cody, it says *'From Angel'* on it."

"C'mon, let's go tell the others."

Diamond was determined to be the bearer of good news. "Come over here, everyone! Look what just happened!"

Tige and Betsy got there first.

"I smell food!" Tige held the bag open and looked inside.

Betsy reached into the backpack and pulled out a thermos filled with something, then a bag containing fourteen ocean-trout filets fully cooked and still warm. Tige grabbed the thermos, opened the top, and slowly breathed in the aroma. It was obviously some sort of soup, perhaps an ocean gumbo.

They continued, pulling out vegetables and fresh fruit, presumably from the island. The backpack also contained plates, eating utensils, and a used pair of size 9 women's tennis shoes.

Victor and Parker joined them. "So, where did you get this?"

Everyone stared at Parker who smiled but said nothing.

"Can one of you answer my question?" Victor insisted. "Where did this come from?"

Cody showed them the alarm clock. Tige read the words on the face which were handwritten with a marker. "From Angel? Who in the *sweet by-n-by* is Angel?"

"Unknown," Cody responded. "But whoever this Angel is, he's one heck of a packer. Look at all this stuff."

Victor walked around behind everyone and scanned the area. "So where are the other bags?"

"This is the only one we found," Diamond answered.

"*Ha!*" Victor snickered. "I've loaded a lot of these 8150 combat packs. It's one of the smaller ones, designed for short missions, light travel." He looked again at the assortment of items which had supposedly come from the bag. "There is no way this much stuff can go in one of these."

Parker spoke up. "So, maybe we should hear it from the beginning. Which one of you lovebirds wants to go first?"

Cody and Di looked at each other. Cody responded to the question. "Lovebirds? Well, I dunno if . . . I mean —"

Diamond interrupted. "So . . . Cody said this, like, prayer thing? You know?" She looked around. Everyone had a blank expression. "I mean, he didn't really think . . . I mean *I* didn't really know if . . ." She shook her head. "So like, he asked God to maybe send an angel with some food. That's what happened. Yep. There it is. That's what happened."

"Who cares?" Betsy raved. "I'm starving!" She reached for a bag.

Tige swatted her hand away. "Not so fast! Before we eat this, I want to hear it from Cody. What exactly happened?"

Cody looked at Parker, who nodded for him to go ahead.

"Di's right. That's all I can tell you."

Parker finally weighed in. "Before we eat this, I think we should thank God Almighty for the provisions. Cody, you should do it."

Cody put his arm around Diamond's shoulders. "I think Di should do the honors. She's the one who thought of it."

Diamond's body language and sudden frown spoke loud and clear — she wanted to hide somewhere. "You want *me* to pray? But I'm the last person who should . . . I mean . . . well, maybe just a short little prayer?"

"Go ahead," Cody whispered.

"How should I do my hands?" she whispered back.

He dropped his head and closed his eyes. "You'll do fine."

Everyone bowed their heads; even Victor, albeit awkwardly.

"So, okay, God . . . I'm like, *so* freaked. I mean, I was never so surprised in my life . . . It's too good to be . . ." She put her fingers over her lips, then she and Cody stared at each other.

Betsy had finally had enough. "Let's eat! I thank God, whoever that is, and the angel, whoever that is! I don't care if the food came from space invaders or Cookie Monster. Let's eat this stuff before we become ghosts!"

She dug in. Everyone else followed.

After the scrumptious meal, everyone had a few moments of lighthearted conversation. Such had been in short supply since the crash.

"Time to talk strategy," Cody said,

Everyone became quiet.

Cody breathed deeply. "I know we have lots of unanswered questions. I'm going to say a few things, then if you wanna ask questions, fire away."

"Wait," Tige said. "I'd like to know what you and Di were really doing out there. Where did you disappear to?"

Diamond responded before Cody could even open his mouth. "We went outside the back entrance to visually survey that area. We're trying to figure out where we are and how we'll get back home. I might as well tell the truth. We were also talking about some personal things. Just talking. Okay?"

Tige grinned. "Good for you, Di." She looked at the others. "We understand, don't we everybody?"

Parker grinned at Cody, but no one else reacted.

"Okay, people. I remind you that bodies lie on the beach. Surely some are buried at the edge of the reef out there in the airplane. We still have no clue as to the power that brought us here."

Every face sobered.

"First, we will refer to this unknown island as 'X-Ray.' This main chamber of the cave will be called 'Alpha,' the waterfall area will be 'Bravo,' and the back exit will be called 'Charlie.' In an emergency, that will simplify our communications."

"Cody, I never did debrief you," Victor said. "Tell us what happened in the cockpit just before the crash."

"Fifteen seconds before the crash I regained partial control, but it was too late. We lost power in both engines and all I could do was try to level off the plane so it wouldn't hit the water in a steep dive. That's the only reason we survived. I wish everyone had made it, but . . ." Cody caught another deep breath.

"I think that whoever was controlling the aircraft wanted us to live. I suspect they were trying to land this plane remotely somewhere on this island. I believe they have some use for us. More than likely, their guidance control technology failed because of the storm, and manual control was partially restored. Whatever they were trying to do went terribly wrong."

Victor picked up the empty backpack and began examining it carefully. He glanced over at the food containers and other items which had come from the empty bag, then shook his head once more in disbelief.

Diamond had a question for Cody. "When they questioned Tige and Betsy, they wanted descriptions of other survivors. Could they have been looking for just one particular person?"

"That's possible. But if that's the case, why not just send somebody to abduct that individual instead of wasting resources on such an elaborate plan? This makes no sense. A remote hijacking would be too expensive."

Victor looked up, still holding the backpack. "They may have been testing the technology. If they could successfully commandeer a commercial flight and land it somewhere remotely, they could hold the entire airline industry hostage."

"That's a plausible explanation. Maybe they want to find other survivors in order to eliminate witnesses."

Di's voice sounded hoarse. "In other words, they might want us all dead?"

Cody nodded. "We have to consider that. These guys are brutal, judging from the way they treated Tige and Betsy."

Tige had a question. "Is anyone looking for us? I mean like Coast Guard or anyone else who might rescue us?"

"I doubt it. The aircraft fell from over twenty thousand feet. It levelled off and flew at three hundred feet the rest of the way. Communications, transponder, and sat-trace functions no longer worked. The aircraft went dark. ATC probably thinks we crashed off the coast of Venezuela. That's how it would've appeared on radar."

Betsy spoke up. "Decades ago, wasn't there some famous incident similar to this? Some foreign airliner from Malaysia?"

"That's right. A Malaysia Airlines flight from Amsterdam to Kuala Lumpur disappeared over the ocean, and . . . well, it was never found."

A dismal silence followed.

Betsy finally broke the quietness. "What about something called ELT? I heard someone use that acronym somewhere."

"It's called Emergency Locator Transmitter. The ELT activates when a plane crashes. It's battery-powered and lasts only a few days." Cody frowned and crossed his arms. "Years ago, satellites stopped listening for ELT signals. So, the only hope for rescue comes if another aircraft flies close enough to hear the ELT emergency signal."

"Are you ex military? I mean, for someone so young, why aren't you still in the service? Something doesn't seem right. You ask us to trust you, but you won't even tell us who you are."

"So, what must I do to win your trust?"

Tige responded. "Cody, tell us your last name. Why be such a mystery man? Maybe you're the person they're looking for."

"Yeah!" Betsy piled on. "I bet Di knows your last name."

"Tell us who you are!" Tige insisted again.

Cody lowered his head and gritted his teeth. "I have reasons for —"

"Now listen to yourselves!" Diamond interrupted. "You should be ashamed! This man risked his life for both of you, and he's just as mystified as the rest of us."

Betsy wasn't to be deterred. "Listen to us, Di. You're partial to Cody for obvious reasons. Granted, he's a beast, and he rescued us, but there is no reason to hide his identity from us."

"Okay, okay," Cody said. "You're right. My last name is Musket."

"Cody Musket?" Tige perked up. "Like the famous baseball player?"

"He's my dad. He's fifty-five years old."

"Now, that explains it," Betsy said. "Your mother is Brandi Musket. 'Mama Brandi' they call her. She's the one who runs all those halfway houses for kids. I admire your mother, Cody. It's just all the hocus pocus God stuff I can't handle."

"Cody, take a look at this." Victor handed him a folded envelope. "I found something in this backpack that got overlooked. How much do you know about this *Angel* character?"

Cody unfolded the small envelope and read a message. "*Sir, I am Angel. I will be in touch. I must return home now to avoid the rain.*"

Betsy jumped all over it. "So, let me get this straight. You said this magic prayer and this errand boy from heaven shows up, then has to get back home before it rains?"

"Yeah," Tige said. "What a shame if the poor angel gets his feet wet!"

"Just hold on a second." Cody held up his hands. "This message may be written in a code, for all we know. Give us time to evaluate it."

Victor agreed. "Whoever this person is, he or she knows we're here and brought goodies we needed. If this Angel person wanted us dead, we'd all be dead."

"Right. If Angel were an enemy, this place would be crawlin' with hostiles by now." Cody handed the message to Betsy. "Pass it around. Let everyone see it."

"For what it's worth," Victor followed up, "I think we should take turns watching the back door."

"Agreed," Cody said. "I'll take the first watch."

The meeting broke up. It was the middle of the afternoon, the second day since the crash.

Cody put a weapon under his belt and went back to the place where he and Diamond had sat underneath the palms. He wouldn't let even an angel go by unnoticed this time.

In a few minutes, he looked up and saw Diamond coming through the exit. She walked over and sat across from him on the ground. "So I guess Angel wasn't an angel after all. Honestly, I'm a little disappointed. I had hoped it was true."

Cody's smile was undeterred. "I see it another way."

"Okay. I'm listening."

"We got more than we asked for."

"Explain."

"Yeah, so, just think about it. Everyone's stuffed and there are leftovers. And what about the shoes? Women's size nine — you and Betsy don't have to share anymore. How did he know we needed one pair that size? Besides that, the amount of stuff we pulled from that bag won't fit."

"So, you think Angel actually came from Heaven?"

"No, but the cubic centimeters don't add up."

"Granted," she said. "There's no explanation for the centimeters. So, what does it mean?"

"Angel isn't from Heaven. He's an ally living on this island. Don't you see? He'll have answers to our questions. Altogether, we got way more than we asked for."

"What about those two prisoners in that hole? Are you still going to interrogate them? Burn 'em with those collars 'til they talk? That's what they would have done to my friends."

"I've never done that," Cody said. "Parker's gonna give 'em food and water. I wanna hear what Angel has to say before we tear into those guys."

"So, fill me in about the dangerous work you do. How can you be the kind of Christian you want to be and an avenger at the same time?"

"I would rather be an evangelist, not an avenger in the traditional sense. If I use force, I'm just trying to level the playing firld, that's all. We're trained to help defenseless victims or protect people we love, *not* to satisfy some primitive animal instinct to get revenge."

"Sounds like reciting an oath. So where does justice enter the picture? Shouldn't we harm those two prisoners in equal measure to what they did to others?"

"No. That's revenge. Those guys are no threat to us now. It's up to the law to dispense justice." He leaned back against the wall and shook it off. "I'll admit the line gets muddied sometimes. I struggle with it, especially where there's no law."

"But sometimes people never get what they deserve. How does that level the field? Maybe the law and God need help dispensing justice."

Cody's fists tightened, then he softened his eyes. "When people don't trust God to do the punishing, they try to do it themselves, and even if they are successful, they just prolong the sorrow. Revenge feels good at first, but it doesn't help you sleep better at night and it can haunt you forever."

They sat in silence for a moment. Cody closed his eyes as a silent breeze ruffled his hair.

"A man who can control himself is mightier that a general who takes a city," he said.

Diamond moved forward and sat beside him. She stroked his sandy blond hair and his unshaven face. "Then, you may be the mightiest man I have ever met, Cody Musket. I can see you do not enjoy hurting people. But you want justice as much as anyone, and that conflict injures you in the deep places of your heart."

With a reticent smile he stared at his own reflection in her soft, shimmering eyes. "So, am I hearing the *real* Diamond Casper? One who's quietly eloquent when she's not acting? The one who can read what's in someone's heart? You're more real than you give yourself credit for."

"Cody, tell me what you felt when I kissed you on the beach before you went to save my friends. Did it mean anything? I just need to know."

He closed his eyes in deep thought. "I had a mission. My only thought was, 'Musket, this is no time to lose your heart.'"

"You *always* have a mission, Cody. So, have you ever lost your heart?"

"Once."

"Can you tell me about it?"

"It was when you kissed me, then handed me your shoes for a friend."

"Well, shame . . . on . . . you for being human. Would you like to know when I lost my heart for the first time?"

He made eye contact but said nothing. She looked away, hoping her face would not blush.

"So, I was on this plane one night about to crash in the ocean, and this brazen guy told me to sit down and shut up and help him find some book to fly the plane with." A measured smile emerged from her parched lips.

"Sounds familiar," Cody replied. "Was I there?"

"You looked at me, just like now, and saw me as a person of worth. I'm good at reading men's eyes, Cody. Most men look at me as if I were a toy to play with."

"So . . . we've known each other only two days. I may always have a mission. Not much room for anything else right now."

"I wouldn't want you to be anyone else. But, I must be honest about something. It troubles me to tell you this, Cody, because I care deeply for you." She took a long pause. "I haven't let any man . . . touch me . . . I mean, not since I left my father's house. I'm not sure that I can. Ever again."

"That will change. You will be whole again."

"Whole *again?* Cody, I have *never* been whole. It took this crash, this island to teach me that."

A breeze moved the palm leaves that shadowed the spot where they sat, allowing a single ray of sunlight to flash through Diamond's hair. Something caught Cody's attention.

"So, what are these yellow flakes in your hair?"

"Cody, what are you talking about? Changing the subject?"

"Seriously, lemme have a closer look." He ran his hand through her dark hair. "Where did you pick these up?"

He opened his hand. It was covered with shiny yellow flakes.

She glanced at her own hand. "Look, I have them on my hand too. I must have gotten them out of your hair when I was . . ."

"The waterfall," he said. "We both had showers this morning. Maybe it's in the water. Let's go check!"

"But why are we just now seeing them?"

"*Unknown, ma'am.* Maybe we weren't looking."

"That's not funny anymore, *sir.*"

They rushed back to the waterfall. Cody grabbed a mug and took a water sample from the falling stream, but they saw no gold.

"It's too dark in here." Di took the cup. "C'mon, let's go look at this in the sun."

They headed back to the outside with the water sample. The direct sunlight revealed thousands of tiny gold flakes floating in the mug.

"Cody! Do you think this is gold?"

"Looks like it to me. Gold has become scarce. But if this is gold, it means we need to strain the water before we drink."

"But I wonder if gold has anything to do with the secret activities on this obscure island?"

"Good question," Cody said. "Pure gold is safe to consume in small quantities like this, but if it has traces of copper, it can be toxic."

"How do you know all this?"

10

ANGEL

Twenty-three years earlier
Country of Librador

The exodus had just begun. Cody, Brandi, fourteen rescuers, and thirty-nine children faced impossible odds. Capistrano's rogue army of hardened fighters was in pursuit. With no provisions, isolated from the world, their prospects were grim. Soon, a disturbance arose among the children at the rear.

"Paco! Paco! Come back!"

Six-year-old Paco had run off. The kids had tried to call him back, and several had run after him. Chavez, Cody's tactical commander, held up the march and scrambled to the rear. Paco, the traumatized child whose brother had been shot earlier, had stripped off most of his clothes and had taken off like a gazelle into the jungle.

"¿Por cuál camino se fue?" Chavez asked. They all pointed into the jungle in the direction Paco had fled. The few who had run after him were panting. They declared that Paco was way too fast to catch.

Brandi and seven-year-old Knoxi stood together looking at

the youngster's clothing lying on the ground. "Why did he run off, Mama? Where's he going without his clothes?"

"He witnessed his brother shot this morning," Brandi told her. "He's really sad, not thinking straight."

"What's your plan, Chavez?" Cody wanted to know.

"I vote we try catching him, but it's *your* call. I don't wanna lose any more kids, but we don't have any time to waste. Capistrano isn't going away."

"Why did he leave his clothes here?" Brandi was confused.

"My guess, ma'am? It's because he's traumatized. No telling what some of these kids have been through."

"We're goin' after him," Cody said. "Let's gather up his clothes. He's bound to be tired, and he can't go far with no shoes — not on this stuff." He pointed to the rocky ground.

"Okay." Chavez pulled together a search team. "Dakota! Hampton! Seaman! You're with me!"

"Here are his clothes, Mr. Chavez." Brandi handed him Paco's things. "You think you can catch him?"

"In answer to *your* question, ma'am, Dakota is the best tracker here, and Joe Hampton and Lefty Seaman are former rangers who know this sort of terrain. We'll find Paco. Just hope he hasn't fallen into a hole or quicksand."

Knoxi reacted, "*Ohhh*, roger that." Her tearful eyes caught Brandi's attention. Brandi picked her up.

"Babe, you and the rest stay here and guard the kids," Chavez advised. "Make sure they keep their heads down. If you don't hear from me in thirty minutes, start everybody moving again. We'll catch up."

"Copy that," Cody nodded. "Thirty minutes."

They circled the area, looking and listening, but found no sign that Paco had been there. Dakota stopped in his tracks. His well-tuned sense of smell detected the odor of human urine. One of the tall acai palms began to drip around the base. He looked upward.

Paco was frozen, clinging to the trunk approximately thirty feet up, hugging it with arms and legs that shook with fatigue.

"How did that tiny kid get up there?" Chavez stared.

"I dunno," Dakota said." He's about to fall. He can't hold on much longer."

"Yeah," Hampton agreed. "He won't be able to come down on his own. Gimme a hand!"

Hampton began shimmying up the tree, using the webbing between his feet to push himself upward. He looped the second strip of bark around the tree as a safety belt and used it to pull himself toward the boy, sliding it upward as he went.

Paco began to slip. Hampton was still seven feet shy of reaching the exhausted child. "He's gonna let go! Gonna fall!"

When Paco let go, Hampton made a valiant effort to catch him, but the sweaty youngster was slippery, difficult to grasp. The petrified boy slipped through Hampton's grip, but somehow managed to latch on to Hampton's ankle with both arms. Hampton carefully slid down the trunk of the tree with the child holding on. Both came away with only minor scrapes.

The four men cleaned Paco up. One side of his face and neck was still spattered with dried blood. His brother had been shot while running next to him during the escape from the compound earlier that morning. In the rush, no one had noticed the dark red spatters on his face until now. His feet had a few cuts from running over the rough ground, but were heavily callused. This kid was used to running barefoot on hard surfaces.

Paco said nothing. They could only guess what country he was from and what he had been put through. Paco showed no emotion and displayed what soldiers call the "thousand-mile stare."

"This kid's definitely a climber," Hampton said. "There are some tribes about two hundred miles from here in the center of the forests that survive by climbing trees to get the fruit. They work naked. He may be from that region."

"Yeah, he seemed to know what he was doing," Chavez said, as he helped Paco put on his t-shirt, pulling it down over his head and onto his bony frame. Then Chevy lightened up and asked the boy a question, grinning and rattling off some Spanish, but Paco was still unresponsive.

~   ~   ~

Present day, Island X-Ray

"Cody? Cody, are you awake? I have something to tell you."

Cody opened his eyes. "Is the sun up yet?"

"Not yet," Diamond whispered. "I want to tell you that I borrowed your socks this morning."

"You did what? My socks? Are you stealin' my clothes again?"

"No, I got them off the floor where you left them. I washed them thoroughly and used them to strain the drinking water."

"What? You mean everyone has to drink water strained through my socks?"

"Tastes great! I'll just tell everybody it's bad coffee."

"Very funny," Cody yawned. "Is anyone else awake?"

"Victor's watching the back door. He took over after your shift." She held up his wet socks. "Take a look. I strained enough water to fill five mugs, but your socks have no gold in them."

Cody sat up. "So, the gold in the water is intermittent. Hmmm. That's unexpected."

"I wonder if this Angel person will come today. Maybe he or she can fill us in. Here are your socks."

"Yeah, I have one more pair in my carry-on which I managed to recover. Uh, how's your sore shoulder and the other scrapes and bruises?"

"The scrapes still bother me a little, but my shoulder wound isn't infected. Parker did a good job sewing me up."

"Yeah, that old man's still got it."

"Something else, Cody. I . . . Don't laugh, okay? I prayed to God last night after you went to bed."

"Okay. So, what did you and God talk about? If it's any of my business."

"I tried to believe in Jesus."

"Okay. Anything else?"

"I asked Him to reveal Himself if He's really there, but I didn't feel the agape love you talk about. Is that when you're supposed to feel it?"

Cody chuckled. "Come here." She sat down next to him. "You took a positive step. You're going the right direction. You might be surprised by what happens next."

"By the way," she said. "I had this crazy dream this morning. I was in a black airplane with two blond teenage girls."

"I guess livin' in a cave does crazy things to your mind sometimes. Your two friends are blond, but they're not teenage girls."

She changed the subject. "You want some leftovers from yesterday? We have some fruit and veggies left."

"Yeah. I'm gonna have to interrogate the prisoners if this Angel person doesn't get here. We need to burn those bodies on the beach, but it may not be wise to leave this cave until we know more." He munched down on a juicy giant pear.

Victor approached Cody. "One of the prisoners wants to talk to you. He won't talk to anyone else."

"Well, maybe I'll get some answers sooner than we expected. I'll head down there after I drink a mug of Di's coffee brew."

~   ~   ~

Cody and Victor dropped a rope into the lower chamber where the two prisoners were being held. The younger of the two took hold. Cody and Victor pulled him up. They secured his hands with a length of roped used earlier to tie the hands of Tige and Betsy after they had been abducted.

"What's your name, or should I say, what shall we call you?" Cody asked him.

"Uh, my name is Vance Carter. That's actually my real name. I'm from Panama City but I'm an American."

"I understand you have some information for me. Let's go around the corner to the waterfall."

Cody led Carter to the area where the water was falling into the reservoir. It made a steady, cool, splashing sound. Carter was near Cody's height at around 5'10", with light brown hair, handlebar mustache, broad shoulders, and a scar underneath his left ear. His hands were burn-scarred but fully functional, and his right eye squinted.

"You wanna take a shower? Might wanna leave your boxers on cuz they could use a shower too. Those mugs are there if you want a drink. There's plenty o' water."

"Thanks for the hospitality," Carter said. "I didn't expect that."

Diamond had tiptoed up near the shower area to eavesdrop. She couldn't resist.

The young man took a long drink and then stepped underneath the water flow.

Cody leaned against the wall. "So, before we get started with the important stuff, tell me about the water. Got any idea where that water you're drinking originates?"

"Comes from up the hill. There's a mountain behind this cave. The water has gold particles in it. Pure gold."

"Pure gold? Is that supposed to impress me?"

"We had it tested. It's as pure as a diamond mist in Montana. Lotta people claim it helps arthritis and skin rashes. We both know that ain't true, but with the gold shortage, they'll pay 'bout $4900 an ounce for these flakes."

"Sounds like a profitable business for someone with red-hot initiative and ice-cold fingers. Is that what your bosses use child laborers for? To strain out all the flakes? Good source of free labor, right?"

"Look, the only ones who can afford the gold are those rich Japs and greedy Jews. And, about the kids; they come from the streets. They'd be dead already if we didn't have 'em here."

"Is that a fact?"

"Look, I wasn't the one who shot the bodyguard. I think you

should know that."

"I do know that, Mr. Carter. I checked the Tokarev you carried. It hadn't been fired. But you were an accessory to the murder of a good man who was brought here against his will."

"Already have me convicted? You ain't gettin' off this island in one piece unless you listen to what I came to say."

"Okay, so why did you want to talk to me?"

"I have no idea who you are, hero. But my bosses will pay you ten times what you're making right now. A man with your skills could go a long way if you hook up with us. We're the future in this region of the world."

"That's something I might consider. When could I get a tour?"

Parker ran into the room and whispered in Cody's ear. "Angel just showed up."

Cody shielded his mouth. "Tell Victor to keep Angel out of sight 'til I put Carter back in the hole. Angel might be an infiltrator, and we don't wanna blow his cover."

"Understood." Parker left the room.

"Okay, Carter, let's go," Cody said. "Hope you enjoyed the shower and the gold-flaked water. We both found out what we wanted to know."

Diamond quickly disappeared so that Cody would not know she had been listening.

Cody returned the prisoner to the hole. As he prepared to meet Angel in the front chamber, he saw Diamond coming toward him.

Cody spoke first. "Well, did you hear everything you hoped to hear?"

"Cody, please tell me you aren't thinking of playing a shell game with these guys."

"Don't worry. That guy's just a drone. He's not authorized to make a deal with me. He was just sizing me up. You want to meet Angel?"

"You mean I can go with you?"

"Why not? It's better than eavesdropping."

Cody and Diamond scurried anxiously toward the main chamber of their hideout. The heartbeat of anticipation grew with every step. In a few moments, they would put a face with the name on the clock. Would this be a game-changer?

When they walked into the cavern's front chamber, Victor and the man calling himself Angel were steeped in animated conversation in Spanish. When they saw Cody and Diamond, they stopped abruptly.

Angel was thirtyish, short and stocky, his brown hair thick and curly. His tan face was weathered, his broad chest and bulging legs on display despite wearing dungarees. Two things became immediately apparent: Angel wasn't one who spent much time behind a desk, and yes, he was entirely human. He wore Radian 5 combat boots like those that Cody had confiscated from his two prisoners.

Angel's face lit up when he recognized Diamond. "*Buenas días,* beautiful lady. I see some of your films. You are more beautiful than I imagined. I am so glad you survived the crash, but I am sorry we meet at a time of so much death and sorrow."

Victor turned to Cody with a disquieted face and an edgy voice. "Cody, you need to hear this guy out."

"I am *Angel,*" the stranger announced. "That is codename. My real name is Juan Angel Fernando Roberto Castillo. I am from the province of Andalusia in the country of Venezuela. I am agent for *Candle of Freedom* trying to make liberty for all my people. I apologize I leave so quickly yesterday. I am nearly late to check in and I must get back before the rain because the storm would have slowed me down."

"Understood."

"I need your help, *Señor* Musket."

"You know me? You know my name?"

"Oh, *Señor*, the first time I see you, my prayers are answered. I recognize you from Librador many year ago. I was with your sister Knoxi and other children. We escape. I was called 'Paco.'"

Cody glanced at Diamond whose mouth had fallen open.

"Well, Angel, that was before I was born. But people do say I look like my father."

"I was very sad. My brother Raul die with bullets. I was only six, but I remember. Your father, he is great man. Chevy great man. I want to grow up to set free children like your father and Chevy."

By this time, Tige, Betsy, and Parker had gathered around.

"So, Angel, you have to understand one thing. The information about that event is a matter of public record. Anyone could have memorized all that. So, let me ask you a question. Your dog had three names. Do you remember them? That part was never made public."

"No, Mr. Cody. The only name I remember is the name I give to him. It was *Los Heridos*. It means 'The Wounded,' for all the wounded children who were sad in their hearts. But now they are free, and I am free. I was fast runner. Climb up tree. I fall. They catch me. Chevy comfort me, help all children be free."

Diamond reached for Cody's hand and placed her lips near

his right ear. "I believe him, Cody. I think he's telling the truth."

Cody glanced at Tige and Betsy. They both nodded their heads with positive but somber expressions.

Victor stepped in. "Angel, tell Cody about the children on this island."

"Many children here, sad like me before. They must work. Many die here but no one care." He paused to make eye contact with everyone.

"My country is in ruin. The central government has lost control. Powerful men try to revive my country by taking over businesses, new technology. But they fight poverty by eliminating the poor, and they use the little ones for free labor."

"So, who's running the show on this island?"

"They call their company *La Luz del Cambio*, 'The Light of Change.' They grow bigger and bigger. Soon, they will take over whole country of Venezuela, and then whole continent."

Diamond offered Angel a cup of water. He took a sip, then thanked her politely before continuing.

"They have big operation here. This island very isolated. They activate shield to hide the island from view. Even satellites cannot see. Giant gold and silver deposits here. Largest in the world, but we have no evidence to prove."

Cody frowned. "You mean they can make this island invisible? So where do they get the technology?"

"Five year ago they kidnap four top scientists. No one can find them."

"I remember that," Betsy said. "The cases were never solved."

"Yeah, I remember it too," Cody said.

"La Luz del Cambio has plenty gold and silver. They use the

children in mines. Free labor. The make captured scientists create new inventions like technology that bring your plane here."

"Okay, okay, I'm beginning to understand. How did you know we were hiding in this cave, and how did you know who I was?"

"When you rescued these two pretty ladies, I see you with my field glasses from a distance. Me and my compadres have decided we will let no more women or children be captured, on forfeit of our lives if necessary. If you had not been there, I would have rescued them. But I did not want to break my cover."

Victor broke in. "So you saw Cody from a distance and recognized the physical similarity to his father? You must have a good memory."

"Oh, no," Angel said. "Look here in my wallet. I have Cody Musket baseball card. I receive it when I send in Cocoa Puffs coupon."

"So," Cody said, "you and your fighting men have managed to infiltrate La Luz del Cambio and you're working' undercover with Candle of Freedom?"

"Si, that is correct. After we successfully infiltrated La Luz, they assigned us to this island under penalty of death if we reveal its location to anyone."

Cody examined Angel with eye-to-eye scrutiny. "So what will you do if you ever get off this island?"

"I will reveal location to everyone. The freedom of my country is, how you Americans say, 'up for grabs.' The wounded people with sad hearts are many, but my life is only one."

"Amigo, do you know why they remotely hijacked our plane and brought it here?"

"Si, of course. They want to hijack planes so they can shake down any airline in the world. But so far, the process is only experiment."

Parker jumped in. "So, Angel, you're saying this whole thing was an experiment that didn't work?"

"That is correct, sir. The lightning from the storm must have broken their connection, and the plane crashed in the water. They wanted to land it safely on island to capture alive Thirsty Giant and our beautiful film star."

Cody bristled up. "Film star? You mean Di? Why did they want her?"

"Because of film *Land Without Shame* which will expose corruption of La Luz and many government officials."

"Thirsty Giant?" Parker asked. "Do you know who Thirsty Giant is?"

"No sir, but he is powerful ally of children and was getting too close. He want to, how you Americans say, *'blow La Luz del Cambio operation out of the water.'*"

Cody put his arm around Diamond who now clung to him. "So, why didn't they just abduct Diamond and this Thirsty Giant person off the street? Why the elaborate hijacking?"

"Because capturing Thirsty Giant and film actress with this technology would be big deal. Like Americans say, *'feather in cap.'* It would cause great fear with anyone resisting them. They like to scare people and never show their faces."

"Hmm," Cody mused. "Seems like this Thirsty Giant person is good at scaring bad guys without showing his face either. I'm familiar with him, but I dunno who he is. Was he supposed to be on this flight?"

"Yes, Mr. Cody. But we have no description, so maybe he is dead."

"So, the hijacking would have accomplished two purposes," Victor surmised. "It would have eliminated two enemies and served notice that an unknown entity at an unknown location could remotely capture a commercial aircraft while the whole world stands by."

"Angel, you said you needed our help. What do you want from us?"

"Mr. Cody, another boat with children left Caracas today. It arrives here tomorrow night. We must save those kids. We must stop the boat."

11

PIRATES?

The following morning, Diamond slept late. Cody had departed at daybreak with Angel, who had promised to show him a hidden bunker on the mountainous side of the island. It was a similar cave but was buried much deeper, and was at least triple the size of the one in which they were currently taking refuge. In this morning meeting, Cody, Angel, and his men would devise a plan to stop the boat and save 25 children against narrow odds.

Angel's men had been building up a supply of munitions and survival gear in this alternate cavern. The entrance was even more well-hidden than their current one, and it would make a good place to temporarily keep any rescued children. Food would be a problem, but Angel was determined to find a way for everything.

He had discovered both caves in his mapping of the island — part of his duties as a terrain specialist for La Luz. He had neglected to mention to his bosses the discovery of these two caves and other similar ones.

Diamond arose and made her way to the waterfall. She stood under the water flow for a few minutes, then covered herself with a blanket and sat nearby, watching and listening to the water splash into the small reservoir. Soon, Betsy wandered into the area, wearing a two-piece swimsuit she had found in one of the carry-ons. After her shower, she sat down next to Diamond.

Betsy was 36, single with frosty-blond hair and a body that she took to the spa twice per week. The waterfall would suffice this morning, but nothing could squelch her nebby curiosity.

"I'd pay good money to hear your thoughts, Dibird."

"Oh, my mind was finding a way to relax. Listening to the water is therapeutic, you know."

"You love him, don't you," Betsy concluded.

Diamond could no longer hold back. With one hand, she held the blanket securely around herself. Her other hand covered her eyes, and she began to sob like a child.

"I'm sorry, Di. Everyone can see your heart on full display, and we don't blame you."

"I don't know what's happening to me. I've never seen such selfless people. Angel risks his life to help us. His men are ready to die for children they don't even know. I've always been more concerned about my bra size and keeping my waist down than about the needs of other people, even my friends. What does that make me? I don't want to be this person anymore."

"I see a change in you already, Di. All the Jesus stuff? All the talk about doing unto others? This is not the Diamond Casper we've all loved to hate. And, sweetie, I like the change."

Tige, tall, thin and wiry, her hair bundled in back, found her way into the room. "I couldn't help but hear. Nothing's secret around here, the way sound carries in this place. I woke up early. I heard Angel tell Cody there was another cave underneath this one. He said it's hard to find the opening. It's somewhere behind the waterfall. He said Cody would be surprised about what's down there. Anybody feel like exploring?"

"Oh, that sounds like fun," Diamond said. "That's what we need. It'll get our minds off everything that's going on. Lemme get my clothes on."

The three women each grabbed a flameless flare that Angel had left behind. The inner cavern was too dark to explore without them.

They searched downstream from the waterfall, following the reservoir until the water abruptly disappeared. They stood perfectly still and could hear the water falling at a lower level, but they could not see an opening.

They slowly circled around the spot where the water disappeared. Tige, being always the contrarian, turned and looked the other direction.

"Check it out! I see a rope over there!"

Betsy and Diamond turned around. Ten meters away, a rope hung from above and seemed to disappear into the floor of the cave. The three women walked slowly toward the rope, then stopped to take a look. It was nearly three inches in diameter, its rotting strands ragged with age. The floor underneath their feet had become rocky, more like a traditional cave.

Betsy made the first comment. "Ladies, I hate to mention it, but this looks like ship-mooring rope."

"Yeah," Tige agreed. "I wonder how old it is. I wonder how it got here."

"Well," Diamond said, "I wonder what's at the other end of the rope. It looks tight, like something is suspended at the bottom."

Tige laughed. "Maybe this is where they hung Captain Hook!"

Betsy began to respire rapidly, her torch shaking visibly. "Oh," she said. "What if someone's dead? Like, what if there's a corpse at the other end?"

Tige and Diamond looked around. Their torches cast long shadows past the crevices in the sides of the cavern. The ground ahead had a large dark spot where the rope went through the floor.

"C'mon," Diamond said. "This is why we wanted to explore. Let's see what gives."

A few feet farther, the floor began to make cracking sounds like thin ice breaking. Betsy screamed as she fell through the collapsing surface.

"Betsy!" Tige screamed. "What happened?"

"Are you alright?" Diamond yelled. "Betsy, say something."

Diamond lay down and scooted forward on her belly. She bravely looked over the edge, afraid of what she might see. How far had her friend fallen? She lowered her torch to search below.

Betsy sat about eight feet down on a rocky ledge, her eyes open wide, frozen and focused on an object which was staring her in the face.

"Look!" Betsy screeched.

At the end of the mooring rope, a skeleton hung with a thick noose around his neck. With rotting remnants of clothing, a sword sheath secured around his waist, and wrinkled leather boots on his feet, this guy had been there a long time.

"Bets, are you alright?" Tige yelled. "Bets! Bets! Say something!"

Besty shrieked, "Is it dead?"

"What? Can you move?" Diamond reached forward and took hold of the rope. "I'm coming down to get you." She shimmied carefully down the rope and stopped just short of the ancient mariner's head. "Bets, are you okay?"

Betsy began to chuckle, then lost her breath. "Mercy! Did I ask if it was dead?" She became hysterical.

Diamond eased herself onto the ledge, managing to avoid disturbing the sleeping skeleton. She sat down next to Betsy.

"Betsy, why are you laughing?"

"Boo!" Betsy shouted at the skeleton, then began crowing again. Her laughter seemed to push everyone's comic relief button.

"I hope the dead man had a good sense of humor," Tige said, still looking on from above. "So, how are you girls gonna get outta there?"

Betsy picked up her fallen flare. The rope was too far away to reach. She looked down and could not see the bottom of the pit. She and Diamond were sitting on a narrow ledge overlooking a deep, dark unknown.

"Di! Don't look down. And don't look up either."

Suddenly, they heard movement. Someone or something was scrambling over loose rocks or pebbles at their level just a few feet away. Diamond felt a wave of terror move through her midsection. She moved her flare in the direction of the sound, but what she saw was more shocking and surprising than she had expected.

"Betsy, look over there!"

Two red eyes stared back at them in the light of the flare. What was it? A large rodent? A dragon like in a fairy tale? In a moment, the eyes disappeared but something even more amazing remained. Could it be real?

The ledge widened into a large platform that led into another chamber. With the light of their flares, they could faintly see several more skeletons lying amidst the considerable ruble afar.

"C'mon!" Diamond began to crawl toward the tomb-like chamber. Besty followed.

They could finally stand up and walk into the dark, musty sepulcher.

"Are you thinking what I am, Bets?"

The light revealed rotting wooden chests bleeding out the sides with shiny coins and jewels of every color of the rainbow. Collapsing strongboxes made of corroded metal revealed more of the same.

"I'm not believing this!" Betsy cried. "Tige, can you hear us?"

Victor answered back. "What do you women think you're doing? Come out of there! It's too dangerous! Answer me!"

"Victor, you won't believe what we've found down here."

"Are either of you hurt? Tige came and got me. I brought a rope to pull you out."

Betsy yelled back. "This place is worth jillions!"

~ ~ ~

Angel led Cody inside the cavern on the western side of the island. It was approachable from about 30 feet up the side of a mountain, and it overlooked a secluded cove where pirates may have hidden their ships centuries earlier.

"This cave could hide the children," Angel said. "My position with La Luz del Cambio is to map out the island. I have always been a skilled runner. I was on the Venezuelan Olympic team when I was nineteen. I have run all over this island and I know every hiding place. La Luz does not know about this cave or the one where you are hiding now."

Cody visually surveyed the interior of the cave. "So, how are we gonna stop this boat, Angel? We have no GPS capabilities, no phones. We can't even alert Venezuelan Coast Guard or Caribbean Policia del agua. So what plan do you have?"

"Amigo, the authorities do not care about these kids. La Luz buys them off. So it is up to us."

Cody shoved his hands into his pockets and grumbled. "I've heard that too many times."

"I will arrange a diversion at the hour the boat is near. Here is map of island. This is where they plan to land the boat, but one of my men will assist you to board the boat before it reaches the barrier reef, and to eliminate the three-man crew. You have had Navy SEAL training and should be able to carry out this plan. The boat is old-style landing craft; not very fast, limited communications."

"I wasn't a full-fledged SEAL, but I did go through part of the training. My father has a few associates who were SEALs. They took me under their wing for a few months. Who's your man that I'll be working with?"

"He is here." Angel motioned to one of his men, who responded immediately.

"Hello, sir. I am Jesse Flores. I was with *Buzos Tácticos*, the Argentine Tactical Divers Group, similar to your Navy SEALs. I'm a graduate of your Naval Academy, at your service."

"I'll defer to your experience and follow your lead, Mr. Flores.

"Okay," Flores said. "After we eliminate the crew, we'll bring the boat here to the west side and unload you and the kids on the beach. I'll then take the boat out to deep water beyond the reef and sink it. I'll swim back, maybe two miles."

"So, we make the boat and the kids disappear?"

"Correct. And if our plan goes right, La Luz will not know the kids are missing until they fail to show up at the main compound. Explosions will keep them preoccupied all night. By that time, the kids are hidden in the cave and the boat is nowhere to be found."

"I can see it all depends on speed," Cody said. "We have to eliminate the crew before they have time to alert anyone."

"This is true, Cody. We must board and move silently. One tango will drive the boat and two will guard in back."

"So we board from the back undetected. We hit and splash the two tangos, then eliminate the driver and take over the craft. Textbook."

"Yes, as long as everything is as expected and the kids don't react and give us away," Flores said.

"It won't be perfect. It never is. But we can improvise."

Angel commented. "Mr. Cody, this is what we have been missing. We have only one experience diver on team. With you, we have more capability. La Luz del Cambio make big mistake bringing you here. They 'overplay hand,' as you Americans say."

12

OLD BOATS AND A BEAVER

Cody made his way back to the cave where the others were waiting to hear about the mission plan. But first things first. The women had some news of their own. The dazzling pirate treasure was big news.

The bubbly women told Cody all about their venture into the lower cavern — the old mooring rope, the body of the dead pirate, the chamber containing stolen jewels — all the elements of a great romantic fable of conquest from a bygone era.

Cody had a more subdued response. "Good thing someone wasn't killed. A treasure? Hmm, that opens possibilities which we can discuss later. Of course, no one can spend it here. La Luz probably doesn't know about it because they don't even know about this cave. Angel has made sure of that."

Victor wanted to know about the plan to intercept the boat.

When Cody went over the plan, Victor had a question of his own. "If *La Luz del Cambio* has so much technology, how can we just steal a boat and take it to the other side of the island without their knowledge?"

Cody sat down. "Angel said the electronic shield that keeps this island hidden has a flaw. It interferes with their own surveillance at close range. They can't see anything within five miles of their own coast. The same quirk caused them to lose control of our commuter at five miles. It's also why they didn't know where the crash site was at first. They're tryin' to resolve the tech issue."

"Amazing. So someone could just invade and they'd never know it?"

"Not exactly. The shield disrupts all communications and detection devices, but only within a five-mile perimeter. Beyond that, it's lights out for any invader. That's why they chose this isolated island. It's almost three hundred miles to the nearest port."

"So, they'd have to disable the shield in order to see their own coastline?"

"They could do that, but it isn't likely. They would run the risk of being seen by satellite. Besides, they've gotten complacent. They feel invincible because they don't expect anyone to find this place." Cody took a sip of water. "That's why we have 'em worried." He set the mug down before continuing.

"Angel said they use old-style boats to deliver kids because the slow World War II landing crafts can get within the reef and deliver the kids directly to the beach. The boats are hard to find on the open sea because they paint them with their own black surveillance-resistant coating."

Victor walked a few steps to burn nervous energy. "Sounds like they've found a balance between new world and old world. Nobody would suspect a high-tech company of using such obsolete equipment."

"Exactly," Cody said. "The British did somethin' like that to stop the German battleship Bismarck in World War II. Bismarck was invincible 'til she was attacked by obsolete British Swordfish biplanes. The German high-tech anti-aircraft guns weren't designed to shoot at aircraft that slow. One of the Swordfish put a torpedo right through the rudder, and that was all she wrote for Bismarck."

Diamond raised her eyebrows. "I get it. Sometimes you need to go backwards to get ahead."

He nodded. "La Luz uses an antique De Havilland Beaver bush plane equipped with big floats to carry execs to the continent. Same deal — old antique aircraft won't raise suspicion. They moor it in one of the hidden coves on the north side of this island. If I could get my hands on that Beaver, I could climb above the shield and call my brother-in-law. But even then, we would need a late-model thera-mag or pocsat device to make the call, cuz there's no conventional cell signal way out here."

"Your brother-in-law?" Diamond asked. "Who's he?"

"He, uh . . . that's Knoxi's husband. He's pretty good with electronics. I mean, like stuff even most geniuses don't even understand."

"Well, what can he do? Even if you could contact him, what about the shield? How would he find us?"

Diamond saw through Cody's frown. "Okay, never mind. I get it. It's a secret, right? So, when's the boat with children supposed to arrive?"

"Due to arrive at 2300 hours. Flores and I have a lotta swimming to do tonight."

~   ~   ~

At 2200 hours, Cody and Flores swam to the one-mile marker and hid behind the buoy that served as a proximity warning. The boat would slow down before reaching the reef. That's when Cody and Flores would attempt the takeover of the vessel.

At 2300 hours, they heard several small explosions coming from the island. Angel's diversion was in progress.

The landing craft was late. At nearly midnight, the boat finally came into view. It was unlighted, but Cody and Flores were equipped with night goggles. They were able to remain unseen as the boat slowly passed at a speed of approximately two knots. The sea was calm, although lightning storms could be seen in the distant west. The water was warm as they moved like unseen fish toward the stern of the boat.

Two armed guards were jawing on the back end of the craft. Their weapons were lowered, and the lighted smokes in their mouths would make good targets. Cody and Flores silently tossed their lines upward and secured a hold on the stern with rubber grappling hooks. The takeover was in progress.

They climbed aboard and surprised both armed tangos, making silent work of disarming and disabling them without firing a shot. They dropped the two bodies softly into the midnight waters, alerting no one.

Most of the kids were asleep, although several moaned and sobbed. Cody felt all fear leave his body as he observed what no man should ever have to see. Some of these children looked to be no older than five.

Suddenly, gunfire erupted. Cody returned fire toward the muzzle flash. The unexpected fourth tango who had hunkered down next to the kids had met his fate at the point of Cody's bullet, but not before a frightened child had jumped up in the crosshairs of Cody's gun. The bullet had gone through the boy's head before killing the gunman. Cody froze, then realized quickly that someone else was shooting.

He felt a bullet graze his left arm, then returned deadly fire and killed the driver of the boat. Now, all tangos were down. He suddenly realized that Flores had not fired his weapon. He turned around. The ugly reality of war came to rest squarely upon Cody's shoulders. Flores was dead, and a bullet from his own gun had killed an innocent child.

The red flash of hatred for the men responsible for this tragedy, and the salty taste of sorrow overcame him. He fell to a knee, then looked heavenward. He still had a job to do. Twenty-four screaming children were now in his keep. He arose and made his way through the kids and turned the boat westward toward the cove. Two of Angel's men would be there to mark the cove with flares.

The frightened children were out of control. He turned around to see two boys attempting to jump ship. He rushed to the spot and took the two petrified youngsters into his arms and tried to calm them.

"Listen! I'm here to help you. You will be safe soon. Please trust me." He repeated the words in Spanish twice. Finally, the boatload of children quieted down to a soft hum. It wouldn't take much to turn up the volume again.

He spotted the two flares, but had never driven a landing craft. Flores was the experienced driver. He moved the boat into position and made a hard landing on the beach. The kids screamed again, but Angel's men rushed onto the vessel to remove the children expeditiously.

Some children were afraid to leave the boat and had to be carried off. Most were afraid of Cody, who had accidentally shot one of their own. The men solemnly took the bodies of the child and the heroic Jesse Flores from the vessel.

Parker tore open Cody's shirt, cleaned and bandaged his bullet crease, then bid him Godspeed. The mission was his to complete.

Diamond wanted to board the landing craft to check on Cody, but there was no time. Everyone was needed to turn the boat around so that Cody could head for deep water.

As he steered away in the darkness, lightning flashes were getting closer. Time was critical. Behind him, he heard a familiar voice. "I'll hold a light for you, Cody. Look for the light."

He looked back. The voice belonged to Diamond, standing on the beach throwing kisses.

Cody drove the craft back toward deep water. The boat was lighter now without the children, lessening the danger of running aground on the reef, so he moved along quickly. Finally, after passing the buoy again, he set the charges which would blow the bottom out of the vessel. Detonation would take place in two minutes. He also opened the front hatch to allow water to begin flooding across the floor, in case the explosive charges didn't work for some reason. He wasn't exactly an expert with explosives.

He pulled himself up to jump overboard when his peripheral vision caught movement. A small boy had emerged from underneath a tarp where he had been hiding. He was now running toward the other end of the vessel. Cody ran after him, trying not to traumatize him further. He knelt a few feet from the child and asked him to come. The boy was unresponsive, his little eyes dazed and unfocused.

Cody thought about Paco as a six-year-old child, running and climbing a tree to make the pain go away. Chevy had reached out to him and shown him kindness. Now Paco had become Angel, a freedom fighter for trafficked children.

With time running out on the boat, Cody spoke to the disoriented child in English and Spanish, pulling up his torn sleeve to show the child his bullet wound.

"See, I got shot right here. I'm on your side. You're gonna be a great sailor one day, but right now you gotta swim with me."

He reached out and moved toward the child. The boy allowed Cody to gather him up. Cody jumped overboard holding the boy and swam away at top speed to avoid being too close when the boat exploded.

The explosive charges fired right on schedule, sending the old vessel to a resting place at the bottom of the sea. Cody stopped for a moment to look back before continuing toward the island.

To his surprise the small child began to swim on his own, making a beeline for home. Cody swam beside him, helping him along so the youngster could keep up. The water was smooth like glass. The wind was calm.

But things changed rapidly. Winds began to blow, subtly at first, then lightning flashed from cloud to cloud directly overhead. The distant storms were rolling in sooner than expected. Suddenly, a squall line hit the shoreline with full force.

High-velocity gusting winds became contrary, swirling and hitting Cody and his little companion in the face, vying to push them back out to sea. It was all Cody could do to tread water. The boy began to choke in the waves.

~   ~   ~

Diamond waited on the beach, where she stood waving her flare back and forth over her head. She refused to be tired. When the rains started, she was not deterred. Lightning flashes no longer scared her. He would come. She knew it.

The unabating rain was cold, blinding, bitter. She stood faithfully for three hours. The others who had sat with her earlier had given up. Even Victor said that Cody's chances were near zero after enduring the elements for so long a time.

At 3 a.m. she could no longer lift her arms above her head. *"Oh, God, please don't let Cody die. Please, come take care of this Yourself. Don't send your son Jesus. This is a job for a man!"*

~   ~   ~

When the cold rain lowered the forward visibility to just a few meters, Cody wanted to believe he could go on, but exhaustion was eroding his will. He had pulled the child along trying to keep the boy's head above water, but he was running out of strength and disoriented. Was he still swimming the right direction?

He thought of another Librador story. Brandi had told him about his father standing before everyone when they faced certain death, calling on God, pleading for the lives of 50 children.

But Cody's body begged him to stop swimming. He looked up toward the heavens and saw nothing but darkness. *"Oh, God, is this how it ends? What about this child?"*

~   ~   ~

The time was now 3:35 a.m. Diamond had placed the flare on the ground in front of her as it had begun to flicker. It would need to be recharged. She took one last look toward the ocean. Another bright flash lit up the beach, revealing a ghostly figure with a child in his arms stumbling out of the water.

Then it was dark again. Had she imagined it? She picked up her fading flare. Why would someone be carrying a child?

She ran toward the spot where she had seen the figure with the child. Could it be? She continued moving forward in the driving rain. Lightning flashed again. This time, she stopped. The burst of light revealed Cody lying at her feet motionless. The child beside him was cold and shivering but alive!

"Victor!" She screamed. "Somebody help me!"

Victor called out, "Where are you? I can't see you."

Soon she was surrounded by friends, amazed, all in shock.

~   ~   ~

It was no easy task getting the exhausted Cody up the muddy hill in the freezing rain. They placed Cody and the child by the fire.

"Somebody help me get these wet clothes off them!" Diamond took charge. "They'll get pneumonia! Where did Cody pick up this child? He was supposed be alone. Help me get them warmed up!"

Betsy spoke up. "Now, Dibird, you go over there and let us take care of Cody this time."

"*Ohh-hoo!* You said that you didn't wanna mess with him the other day."

Betsy glanced at Tige, then back at Diamond. "Well, sweetie, we've decided he's not such a beast after all."

"*Ha!* You might wanna rethink that."

Parker examined the child and determined that his lungs were clear of water. He just needed to warm up. Tige and Betsy offered, but when the youngster opened his eyes he began to scream, reaching for Cody.

Diamond wrapped the boy in a blanket, then placed him on Cody's bare chest. The child hushed and closed his eyes. Tige covered them both with a blanket.

Diamond's arms and shoulders ached from waving the flare. She shivered from the cold rain, her own clothes dripping wet, but right now she needed only one thing — to be alone so she could cry her eyes out. She ran into the darkest part of the cavern and fell on her face, trying to understand.

Powerful forces of nature had opposed her on the beach. She should have been freezing, but she was warmed. She should have given up, but faith had come alive in her. Could she have just imagined it? She would keep it to herself. It wouldn't do for the others to think she was delusional.

Moments later, after the others had settled underneath their own blankets, Diamond returned. She uncovered Cody's left arm and rewrapped the bullet crease.

She lay down beside the sleeping Cody and the exhausted child, who could not have been more than five years old. She pulled a blanket over herself and nestled her head next to Cody's right arm, then placed one hand on the back of the child. He was warm, soft, and breathing. How in the world had Cody managed to bring this child through the storm? *Is this what it means to invade the impossible?*

13

WHAT NOW?

When the sun rose, the rain was gone and Cody was still asleep. The child who had nearly met his end at midnight had crawled off Cody's chest and was sleeping soundly at his side. Parker took a peek under the blanket at Cody's left arm. He noticed that Diamond had cleaned and rewrapped it the night before. The bullet crease was minor, but without antibiotics it might become troublesome. Angel had promised to provide more med supplies.

Victor's twisted knee had improved. He decided to walk to cave number two where the children had been taken. He would ask Angel about getting medicine.

At noon, Cody and the child woke up. Diamond knew the boy would be hungry and had prepared a veggie soup. The youngster took to Diamond immediately, especially since she was the one handing him the spoon.

"We took your clothes again last night," she teased as Cody came around. "It's getting to be a habit."

Cody took a quick glance underneath the blanket. "Yeah, just don't let it go to your head." He cleared his throat. "Looks like you've made a friend with the little guy."

"Oh, you should have seen him last night. He wouldn't have us. He's obviously bonded to you."

"Yeah, kind of works both ways." He patted the boy on the head. "He's a heck of a fighter, and you should see him swim."

They were quiet for a minute as Diamond helped feed the boy.

Cody's dead exhaustion was obvious even through his amiable smile. "I know what you're gonna say. You prayed to God again last night."

"How did you know?"

"I figured."

"I thought you weren't ever coming back. I asked God to come Himself. I asked Him to not send Jesus. I told Him this was a job for a man."

"You did what? You actually told the Almighty to leave Jesus at home?"

"Well, you said to just tell Him what's in your heart, didn't you? Do you think I offended Him?" She waited. "Cody! Why are you laughing so hard?"

"God was probably delighted," he rasped. "That prayer was pure honesty."

"I thought I was going to lose you. I was desperate."

Cody sat up. "By the way, has anyone seen Angel? His diversion worked last night. I'm hoping he didn't get caught. He took a big risk."

"He hasn't been here. We expected him earlier. Victor went to the other cave to find him. We need antibiotics for your arm."

The brief gleam in Cody's bleary eyes faded. "Flores is dead. And . . . there was this little kid . . . He got in the way when I pulled the trigger . . ."

"We know, Cody. We know. We're so sorry." She rubbed his shoulder. "It was no one's fault except those men who . . ."

"I need to find Angel." Cody bit down hard. "The honchos at La Luz are bound to be suspicious. Their kids and their boat are missing along with those four gunslingers we . . . eliminated last night. They'll be searching everywhere."

"Now listen, Cody. Your arm's infected and you're exhausted. Let someone else take the lead for a day. Mr. Parker thinks the water here might have antibiotic properties. You need to get in that shower. We should also bathe this boy. C'mon, let me help you up."

Cody raised himself to his feet but his knees were wobbly. She placed a blanket around him and supported him as he made his way to the shower. The child walked beside them.

Diamond looked down at the tiny survivor. "Cody, can you ask this child what his name is?"

"I tried last night, but he never said a word." Then he spoke to the child again. "Hey, little guy, can you tell me your name? Where are you from?"

The child looked at Cody but didn't respond.

"Has he said anything? Anything at all?"

"Not a single word, but I think he understands what we're saying. I'm gonna call him Buddy for now."

"Mr. Parker!" Diamond shouted. "Can you please come help Cody and Buddy in the shower?"

~   ~   ~

After Parker had assisted Cody and the boy in the shower, he accompanied them while they walked back from the waterfall. Cody limped slightly, not certain how he had injured his knee.

Perhaps he had twisted it during the operation to stop the boat. His superficial shoulder wound burned. Diamond joined them again as they arrived at the main chamber.

"I'm concerned about Angel," Cody said. "He should have contacted us by now."

Diamond filled him in. "As I said earlier, Victor went to the other cavern to find him. I'm expecting him to report back here within the hour. No one wanted to disturb you this morning."

"I need to get hold of a late-model thera-mag handheld device and contact my brother-in-law. But I need to get above the shield in order to contact him."

"So then, all you need to do is steal that plane and find a thera-mag satellite phone to make the call," she chuckled. "Cody, listen to yourself. You nearly drowned last night, you're limping as we speak, and you've been shot. Stealing an airplane from an army of well-armed psychopaths should be a piece of cake, right?"

"You shudda been an actor," Cody said. "You have a way of sayin' things." He sat on the blanket where they had slept. Buddy sat on his lap.

"Cody, that's twice you mentioned calling Knoxi's husband. What can he do?" She sat down in front of them.

"Ryan is . . . let's just say he's well-positioned. He's with the DOD."

"Your sister has been a hero of mine for years. The way she escaped in Librador, the people she's helped. I never knew she had such a hot younger brother. If my family roots were as noble as yours, maybe my life wouldn't be such a waste."

"We aren't always the sum of our ancestors," Cody squeaked hoarsely. "I mean, even if you have inherited less-than-honorable roots, you can establish your own. You can break the cycle of evil in your family."

"You're talkin' way over my head. Cycle of evil? Grow my own roots?"

"You mentioned *bad karma* yesterday. Karma's a mystic concept that says your past existence determines your future. Jesus says otherwise."

"I'm listening, but I'm not hearing you."

"What I'm sayin' is, you aren't doomed to be the product of your environment or your past. I mean, when you reach for God, He starts to change you from the inside, so the person you eventually become isn't the same person you used to be."

She frowned. "I don't think I could ever believe that."

"Okay, so why did you stay out in the storm 'till three o'clock in the morning? I mean, Parker said everyone else had given up on me."

"Honestly, I don't know. I just couldn't let you go. I've never done anything like that before. And . . . when I saw you lying on the beach with this little boy beside you . . . I mean, it was the most exhilarating moment of my entire life. I've never been so emotional." She fought tears again and covered her lips.

Cody turned quiet and reflective. "I didn't think my legs could keep going. I didn't even know if Buddy was still breathing. The rain was so heavy I couldn't see ten feet in front of me. I didn't know if I was even swimming in the right direction anymore." His closed eyelids told her that Cody was re-experiencing the moment in his head.

"When I couldn't move my arms anymore, I saw this . . . tiny flickering light. All of a sudden, I felt sand beneath my feet. I used my last ounce of strength to walk toward the light."

Cody looked up with red, swollen eyes. Diamond met his gaze and tried to quell her goosebumps.

The misty moment ended when Cody chuckled again. "Did you really ask God to come by Himself?"

"Well, this . . . this prayer thing is all new to me. I keep waiting for God to reveal Himself — the agape love like you talked about, but . . ."

"Seems to me that ever since you prayed on your own a few nights ago, you haven't been the same. Everyone's noticed. Do you think the old Diamond Casper would have stood in the cold rain for three hours, waving an electric flare over her head in a lightning storm for someone? Anyone?"

"Cody, if only I were as certain as you. My emotions are so stretched. I don't know what to think." She sighed. "By the way, you talked in your sleep. You said something about a Rosa's Cantina, and not being trained for this."

"Uh, okay. So, Rosa's Cantina . . . it's an organization that . . . deploys an army of Lions led by a Lamb."

"Will you please speak plain English?"

Suddenly, the cavern began to shake. The ground rumbled and continued vibrating for several minutes.

"Earth tremor!" Cody said. "Stay calm."

When the trembling stopped, Victor ran into the area. "Earthquake! Anybody hurt?"

"We're okay."

"I just got back from Cavern number two. A boulder fell and collapsed our back exit after I came through seconds ago. At least I managed to bring some stew."

Tige and Betsy had been near the front entrance. A rockslide had partially blocked the opening. "Thank God you got here. We are starving, and besides that, this place is gonna be history soon."

Parker walked into the area. "We should stay in this section. We're deeper into the mountain here. Earth tremors run along the surface. The deeper we are, the better."

"True," Cody said. "As long as we don't get trapped."

"That concerns me," Victor agreed. "The other cave might be more secure than this one."

"Did you see Angel in the other cave?"

"No. His right-hand man Pablo says Angel is being questioned this morning. La Luz is ramping up their search for survivors. They know we took the kids and the boat last night, but they don't know where we are."

"Yeah," Cody said. "It won't be long before they're all over this place. We can't just sit back and hope they don't find us."

"Angel said these guys have been sitting here all comfy for years in the middle of nowhere. Maybe that's why they have no helicopters or shore-patrol boats here. They didn't figure on needing any."

"Yeah. Like we talked about earlier, they never counted on opposition showing up."

"Right," Diamond said. "They've overestimated themselves."

"But never underestimate an enemy," Victor warned. "All this makes me wonder how long it'll be 'til they employ well-equipped choppers to sniff us out. We need to move fast."

"Agreed. We have an advantage if we take the fight to them now. They won't expect that. How safe is the road to the cavern where the kids are?"

"We should stay put for the rest of the day," Victor replied. "Patrols are out. They're looking for us in this sector of the island."

"Listen to him, Cody." Diamond was adamant. "You need to stay here. Make some strategy, whatever you guys do, but give your body a chance to recover. The first thing I'ma do is get Mr. Parker to look at your knee. I'll be back in a few minutes."

"Okay, I need to chat with him anyway. Ask him to meet us at the waterfall. It should be safe there. I'd like you to join us. Everybody else can chow down on summa' that stew Victor brought from the other place."

"I wish we could communicate from here with the other cavern," Victor said. "But Angel said La Luz monitors all frequencies, and the only system that works on this island is theirs."

"Yeah," Cody agreed. "It would be nice to know what they know. They must have a way of getting information from the continent about earthquake predictions, weather patterns, stuff like that. We don't need to get trapped beneath this mountain. What we felt earlier may have just been a minor tremor for a coming earthquake."

"What about Buddy?" Tige asked. "Should we place him with the other rescued kids from last night?"

"Maybe in a day or so, as soon as it's safe to walk to the other cavern. We'll leave him here with us for now," Cody said. "He needs to recover too. He came back as water-logged as I did. "I'm hoping he'll say something."

Tige and Betsy nodded and grinned at each other when they watched Cody leave the room holding Buddy's hand.

Cody sat down next to the waterfall. A natural bank ran along the sides of the stream, creating a trough about eighteen inches deep. Diamond sat down on the bank holding Buddy, dangling her feet in the cool water while Parker examined Cody's knee.

"I feel a little swelling," Parker said. "Fluid build-up. You were in the drink a long time last night. Your shoulder looks better. Maybe the shower earlier helped. How does it feel?"

Cody ignored the question, looking circumspectly at Diamond and little Buddy. Finally, he cleared his lungs with a deep breath and turned to Parker.

"So, Joe, when were you gonna tell us?"

"Uh . . . tell you what, Cody?"

Cody said not a word. He simply waited, not shifting his eyes away from Parker. Diamond had no clue.

Parker wrinkled his brow. "How long have you known?"

"Was the codename 'Thirsty Giant' your idea or someone else's?"

"It sounds intimidating, you must admit," Parker mused.

"I invited Di to join us because she's the other target."

Parker nodded. "I'm sorry, Cody, and I apologize to you, Ms. Casper. I was going to tell you both when it seemed like the right time. The fewer people who know, the better." He looked at Cody. "How did you figure it out?"

"It makes sense. You knew too much to be just an innocent civilian who happened to be aboard the commuter. They were after you because you're getting too close."

Diamond's shock made her eyes water. "*You're* Thirsty Giant? What's a Thirsty Giant? Why do you have a call sign, or . . . or codename, or whatever?"

"My ancestors were slaves on cotton plantations for several generations in the old South. We of all people know how priceless freedom is, Ms. Casper. I served honorably in the United States Navy, after which I was accepted to Columbia School of Finance."

Diamond pulled off Buddy's shirt and let him splish-splash in the water. "Go ahead, Mr. Parker. I still don't know why you call yourself Thirsty Giant."

"Well," he continued with a chuckle, "I went to work at a major investment firm on Wall Street and soon became acquainted with the name Andre Cupertino."

"The one and only Andre Cupertino? The billionaire?"

"Yes, ma'am. I modeled myself after him. He hired me, and I worked my way up the food chain. Eventually, I became his second in command. Then, I began to see a pattern. The wealthier he got, the more he manipulated financial markets. Millions of innocent investors were ruined, and I was helping to make it happen." He dipped his hand in the stream and splashed his face.

"That's when I asked God to forgive me and turned my life over to Jesus. I resigned and became a minister of the gospel."

Cody added a few details. "Cupertino's under-the-table activities have increased his reach. His political strength makes him so arrogant that he's openly calling for the downfall of western culture."

"That's right, ma'am, and a growing wave of anarchy is the result. It's a gospel of hate. He's skillfully using his money to break the backs of financial institutions and bring legitimate democratic governments down."

"So then, why did you start using a codename? What's *Thirsty Giant?*"

"Twenty-eight years ago, my paternal grandfather who was a truck driver died and left a fortune in gold coins buried on his property. My uncle inherited the land, and when he died it became mine. It flooded that spring, and that's when the coins started literally washing up in the yard."

"You're kidding! Your grandfather must have been frugal."

"Extremely, ma'am. I invested the entire fortune — over twelve million — into derivatives, options, futures, small stocks, commodities. I used every legal technique I had learned from Cupertino. I lived an unassuming life and reinvested all the profits. Believe it or not, I'm now wealthier than he is." He sat down on the edge of the trough. "He's worth eight billion. I'm worth nine."

"*Nine billion?*"

"I know Cupertino's vulnerabilities. I've been attacking his ventures and exposing his fraud. He now has thirty-nine US indictments against him, but no one knows where he is." He splashed his face again.

"The codename Thirsty Giant is to protect my family. No one knows who I am, not even Victor who works for me. For a long time, Cupertino didn't know. But he recently found out that Thirsty Giant is little ol' me, his own protégé."

"I didn't know who you were, either, Joe. But your offer to join with Rosa's Cantina has been well-received in my family."

"I followed you down here, Cody. I was going to introduce myself in Barcelona. I wanted to first see if you were as trustworthy as everyone said. I'm eighty-one, but your life is still ahead of you. I want to pass on the Thirsty Giant fortune to someone who knows what to do with it."

"So, why does Cupertino want me?" Diamond asked. "I can't imagine he thinks I'm that important."

"Because the film you're starring in will expose him. He's paranoid right now. His people are getting sloppy, taking too much for granted. He wants to make an example of you because you're a public figure. He probably thinks it'll scare his own people back in line."

"There's another possibility," Cody surmised. "He might want to make you a convert, use you for propaganda. Who knows?"

"Cupertino is openly calling out the Musket family as enemies of freedom. Little did he know that when he hijacked our plane, he was bringing a Musket to his own shores. Didn't I tell you Satan would overplay his hand?"

"Do you believe Cupertino, himself, is here?"

"Absolutely. La Luz del Cambio is searching this island for me. Cupertino wants to look me in the eye and tell me I'm beaten."

The cavern began to shake once more. The rumbling sounds returned more pronounced this time. The surface of the stream rippled with the vibrations of the bedrock. It continued for about 30 seconds, then ceased.

A sudden odor filled the air. Cody jumped up. "Get your feet out of the water!" he yelled, taking hold of Diamond's arm. "Smell that?"

Cody reached down and pulled the child out of the stream.

Diamond's voice quivered. "Smells like rotten eggs."

"Sulfur," Parker said. "The water may now be contaminated."

14

OVER HERE? OVER THERE?

The sound of falling rock followed the tremor. The cavern went dark. Diamond felt along the ground until she located a flare sitting nearby where she had left it earlier. When she flipped the switch, the flare provided enough light for everyone to see each other, but not much more.

"Sound off!" Cody said. "Is everyone okay?"

"Uch! Over here!"

It was Tige's voice. She had been sitting barely inside the front entry.

Everyone headed toward the sound of Tige's distress call. The opening had collapsed, leaving a pile of jagged rocks and pebbles blocking the entrance. Leafy branches, having fallen, were now mangled amidst the rubble.

They were shut in. Without the flare, the group would be sitting in total darkness. A dusty cloud hung in the air like a vapor of smoke — misty, odorous.

Parker knelt beside Tige, whose right leg was trapped between two rocks. She was fighting back tears from the pain, breathing rapidly.

"Lemme have a look, young lady." Parker examined her leg. It was caught just below the knee, with bleeding cuts covered by bloody dirt and gritty sand.

"Any more flares nearby?" Parker asked. "Gotta have more light. This flare's getting dim."

"I left three of 'em outside the back entrance this morning," Victor said. "They're probably solar-charged by now, but the back entry may be totally blocked too."

"We gotta get those flares." Cody stepped forward and surveyed the pile blocking the opening. "But I have an idea first. Bring me the dim flare."

Diamond, still holding the boy, stepped near and held up the light. Cody grabbed a sturdy tree branch and began slowly moving it back and forth until he could see light on both sides of it.

"Looks like we could start here moving summa' the rock outta the way," Cody said. "It should create a small opening without collapsing the pile on top of Tige."

Victor and Parker moved enough rocks to make an opening large enough for a small child to crawl through. The light was enough to allow limited visibility inside the cavern. Meanwhile, Cody carried the dim flare toward the back entrance to survey the breakdown.

As he walked through the narrow, twisting passage, another tremor struck. This one shook the flare out of his hand and threw him against the side of the tube. He looked up to see rocks and dirt falling in front of him and then sunlight breaking through.

When the shaking stopped, he picked himself up and moved forward cautiously. The flare was toast — smashed, rundown. But a new opening larger than the old had been created. The old one was now blocked. He faintly heard two men whose voices he didn't recognize talking on the outside.

He lifted himself up through the newly-created hole to have

a look. The two individuals down below wore the same type of dungarees and boots he had confiscated from his prisoners. They were approaching slowly with weapons raised, looking cautiously side to side as they walked. The three flares Cody had come to fetch were lying in the sunlight about forty meters in front of them, right in their pathway, but they had not yet spotted them.

He must not let them find those flares. If he tried to get there first, he would be seen, but if the two tangos arrived first and spotted the flares, the place would be crawling with armed hunters within minutes.

He looked in every direction and spotted several more hostiles searching on the far side of the crater. He would need to act quickly and hope no other enemy hunters were in the area.

He dropped back inside the tube and raced toward the waterfall. "Di! Bring me the boots we took off the prisoners."

He shed his green dungarees and began pulling on a gray pair he had taken from one of the prisoners. Diamond approached with a pair of the Radian 5 boots. Buddy was following.

"Cody! What's happening!"

He buttoned the dungarees and began pulling on the boots. "These don't exactly fit, but . . . Tell Victor I'm gonna need his help in a minute, but tell him to stay out of sight."

"Cody, what about your knee?" Buddy reached for Cody, but he didn't notice.

He dashed back to the new breakdown hole and rubbed dirt and grit into his face, hair, and arms. Hoping that Parker's assessment was accurate, that Cupertino's men had become sloppy, he crawled up through the new opening and slid down the hill on his belly, boots-first.

"*Ayuadame! Estoy herido!*" ("Help me! I'm injured!")

The two armed individuals lowered their weapons and ran to assist a fellow hunter who had obviously been caught in a rockslide. When they reached Cody he surprised them both, bashing their heads against the wall before they could react. Cody jerked their coms off their faces so they could not alert anyone, and then pulled them one by one up the ten-foot incline and placed them next to the opening.

Victor helped him lower the two stunned individuals into the tunnel.

"Check these guys for more weapons," Cody said. "Find out if they're wired with homing terminals like the other one. I'm going back to get the flares."

Cody climbed back through the opening, then moved cautiously toward the flat area below. Armed with an assault weapon he had just confiscated, he picked up the solar-powered flares and expeditiously returned to the seclusion of the tunnel.

Victor and Cody placed the prisoners in the hold, then lit up the flares and returned toward the others while discussing their precarious situation.

"Was anyone else injured in that last tremor?" Cody asked.

"We freed Tige from the rock pile just in time. She's got a bad bruise, a turned ankle, and maybe a couple of broken toes. But she's mainly shaken up. She's not talking, just moaning and hyperventilating. Parker and the two women are with her. Your kid is none the worse for the wear."

"*My* kid?"

"Well, that's what everybody thinks. The kid seems to believe it too."

Cody got back to business. "It's a good thing the original rear opening was covered by the landslide. It could have been spotted.

The new hole is harder to see from below."

"I know one thing," Victor said. "This location isn't safe anymore. If we have one more tremor or a full-fledged quake, we're finished, not to mention the danger of being discovered. Plus, we're cut off from the other cave now. It's dangerous to go out there. La Luz is stepping up their search."

"Roger that. It won't take 'em long to realize these two grunts I just apprehended are missing. And if La Luz keeps searching this area they'll discover the other cave too."

"I have an idea," Victor said.

"I'd like to hear it."

"Okay. My Spanish is better than yours, and I'm good at playing 'bad cop,' as they say in your country. I'll make one of the new prisoners report in and tell his bosses there's nothing here, no reason to search longer. I'll have him say that he and his buddy have headed to the eastern side of the island. I'll monitor the conversation on the other com."

"Good idea," Cody agreed. "If La Luz would move their search to that side of the island, we could move our base to the other cave while they're not looking."

Victor had another idea. "We could really make it work if we sneak outta here just before dark and make a guerrilla strike on the eastern side."

"I like your strategy, amigo. They might actually move *all* their guys to that side. They won't know where to look. Over here? Over there?"

15

'GORILLA' WARFARE

Tige had developed a fever. She shook with chills and called for water repeatedly. Her leg wounds were puffy and red. Parker needed antibiotics. They all needed water. The contamination of the waterfall had come as a great blow.

"We may have to delay our guerrilla raid," Cody told Victor. "We need water and medical supplies. How much do Angel's guys have in the other cave?"

Victor's face twitched nervously. "Angel was supposed to bring us water after he returned from the La Luz compound, but they detained him for questioning. I think they suspect him."

"How many people does Angel have to watch those kids?"

"Only about three at a time. They rotate. They have to report for duty with La Luz."

"One of us has to go over there," Cody said. "I'll get that backpack and get started. Any chance you got a map?"

"Lemme go, Cody. I know the way. It's only fifteen minutes."

Cody glanced at Diamond. She folded her arms but would not engage his eyes.

"Okay." Cody gave him a nod. "Go ahead. But I'm gonna listen to their communications with one of the coms. I'll immediately know if you get in trouble on the way."

"Yeah, that'll work."

Eight minutes later Victor was stopped. Cody understood enough Spanish to know they were taking him to the compound.

"I gotta go!" Cody yelled. "Victor's in trouble. He's only a few minutes from here."

He ran past Diamond and little Buddy and headed straight to the exit. When he emerged, he could see Victor and two enemy agents talking near the north perimeter of the crater. Victor used the name and employee number of the individual who had worn the headset, but they knew he was an imposter. The two agents were taking him to the compound for interrogation. Cody hastened his steps to catch up. By the time he had overtaken them, five more hunters had joined them. He had to think of something fast.

He followed until he could see the compound. It was a five-level structure with hundreds of solar panels and few windows. He counted ten more armed men coming down the hill to join a parade that would deliver Victor to the facility.

Navy SEALs had taught him that when a situation looked impossible, do the last thing your enemy expects. Cody had an idea. It was the longest of long shots, a stunt probably never tried before, but it was all he could think of.

He yelled into the headset. *"Gorila! Gorila! Hor un enorme gorilla por aquí!"* ("Gorilla! Gorilla! There's an enormous gorilla over here!") Cody pointed northward toward the sea, which was visible from where he now stood. He made sure he was seen, then started running that direction, hoping to draw enough armed personnel away from Victor that he could somehow escape.

To his surprise, it created a banner reaction from Victor's escort. Everyone headed toward Cody and followed him down the hill toward the coastline. Cody turned a corner and slipped on some loose rock, cutting a gash in his sore knee. He then rolled off the edge of a ridge into a patch of tall grass and scrubby bushes. He watched the entire brigade pass him by. Victor wasn't with them. Had he managed to escape?

He backtracked until he saw one of the soldiers lying face down on the ground, trying to raise his head.

Then he heard someone behind him. "*Psssst!* Over here!"

Cody spun around. It was Victor, who had faked a sprained ankle and had fallen down. The unfortunate individual who had stayed behind to guard him now regretted it.

They hastily proceeded to cave number two, where Angel's men were watching the kids.

"Gorilla? Whatever made you think of that? Can you believe those guys bought your act?"

"I didn't think it would be that easy. I was hoping a few of 'em would chase me. You'd think it was gorilla season by the way they reacted."

"You're weird, Musket. In fact, you're freakin' scary!"

When they walked into the other cave, Angel's men were waiting. They began to applaud.

Pablo Fuentes, one of Angel's fellow infiltrators, introduced himself to Cody. "How did you know about the gorilla?"

"What are you talking about, amigo? I just yelled 'gorilla' off the top o' my head."

Pablo and the others began laughing. "*Ohhh, amigo!*" He patted Cody on the back. "We were listening to you. La Luz has been doing animal research. Godzilla the Third escape this morning. A tremor loosened his cage. They search for him all day!"

Victor stared at Cody again. "Like I said, Gunfighter . . ."

"We have your medicine and more fresh fruit for you." Pablo was still chuckling. "The fruit is all we have today. It will help you watch your waistline, American." He grinned. "You have brought joy and laughter to us, Gunfighter. We are in your debt. We can see that God rides with you. Together we will defeat these banditos and our people will be free again."

"You and your guys are the real heroes, Pablo. And speakin' of heroes, have you heard from Angel?"

"He was questioned this morning. We do not know what happened after that."

"Can we see the kids? I hear 'em but I don't see them."

"Come with me."

Cody tightened his face. "I'm hoping the kids from the boat won't remember me."

"You gotta let that go," Victor said. "Not your fault. Think about the ones who survived."

"If only that kid hadn't stuck his head in the line of fire. It's all coming back, the image in my head . . ."

Cody and Victor followed Pablo around a bend to an even larger cavity and saw the 24 children who had been saved the night before. The scene was more than sobering. The blended sounds of sobbing, muttering, calling out for a mother, one child wailing — was there no one to comfort these children?

"Can't somebody talk to these kids?" Cody turned to Pablo. "I mean, someone should say something."

"Angel has a way with words, amigo," Pablo said. "But the rest of us, we dunno what to tell them. You are welcome to try."

"Buy my Spanish sucks," Cody said.

Victor spoke up. "Give it a try, Gunfighter. It can't hurt." He nudged Cody forward toward the audience of mourning kids.

Cody cleared his throat. "Okay, uh . . . *Mi padre era un gran zopilote in el Cuerpo de Marines de los Estados Unidos.*"

Suddenly the children grew quiet. Some smiled, others laughed out loud.

Cody stopped speaking and turned to Victor with a shocked expression. "What did I say?"

Pablo jumped in, still laughing. "Oh-ho, amigo. That was perfect. You make the children smile."

Victor broke the news to Cody. "Dude! You told the kids your father was a great *buzzard* in the United States Marine Corps!"

"Yeah, that figures. I was tryin' to say *pilot.*"

Victor explained to the children that Cody was not fluent in Spanish, but that a plan was being devised to free them. Most returned to crying, while others stared with empty expressions. These were runaways, orphans, street urchins. They had no place to go even if they were freed. The youngest looked to be about five, the oldest, maybe fourteen.

Cody turned around with clenched teeth. "With God's help, we're gonna get these kids off this rock and help them find a life. No more forced child labor. *Enough!*"

Cody said little as he and Victor expedited their fifteen-minute hike back to cave number one where the others were waiting with great anxiety. Diamond met them in the tunnel near the entrance. She embraced Cody and Victor. Cody's expression was distant. He stayed behind while Victor went into the main chamber to join the others. "See you in a few, Gunfighter."

Cody's face was ghostly, deflated, his lips tight. Diamond had never seen him this way, not even in the cockpit the first night.

"Cody, what happened? Did you run into trouble? Cody? Can

you look at me? Can you tell me?"

Diamond felt his arms reach around her. "I saw the kids. The ones we brought from the boat . . ." His voice weary, hoarse.

She waited, but soon realized she would receive no further explanation. He gripped her tighter and tighter. She felt his heavy breath on her neck. His strength frightened her. At first she felt the urge to resist, but alas she did not want to escape his grasp, and that scared her even more.

He softened his hold. "I'm sorry. I shouldn't have. I mean, sometimes I forget myself . . ." His face remained like flint. "I would never . . . never hurt you."

"I know what hurt feels like, Cody. You didn't hurt me."

As they walked to join the others, Diamond straightened her blouse and tried to arrange her stringy hair. Saltwater, sand, and wind without shampoo and sauna for four days had taken its toll.

When they arrived, Victor was telling everyone his version of the gorilla story. Even Tige laughed, aware that Victor might have embellished the details. Cody chuckled, then sobered quickly.

He scanned the room, but couldn't find what he was searching for. Diamond nodded in the direction where the mute child had finally fallen asleep. Cody followed until he found the boy in a secluded corner. Di had covered him with a blanket.

When Cody lay down beside Buddy, the child latched on.

The connection between Cody and the small boy was palpable. Now Diamond understood; Cody was the strongest man she had ever known, but even he could not fight his battles alone. She wanted to join them, but would she be intruding?

She reclined near them. They fell asleep and did not awaken until the next morning just before daybreak.

16

DO YOU WANT ME?

Diamond was frantic. "Cody! Cody, wake up! Buddy's gone! We've looked everywhere. He's nowhere in the cave!"

Cody rolled over and tried to wipe the sleep out of his eyes. "What are you saying? Did you say Buddy's missing?" He jumped up. "Where did you see him last?"

"I saw him right here last night. He and I fell asleep right here with you. Remember?"

Cody exhaled heavily. "Yeah. Yeah, I remember now. So, how long ago did he disappear?"

"I woke up maybe ten minutes ago and he was gone."

"I'm going out to find him," Cody said. "The sun's coming up. I need to find him before La Luz starts patrolling this area."

"Here are those combat boots you wore yesterday."

"No, no. Those boots don't fit. They hurt my feet. I need my sneakers."

Victor came in, panting. "I already looked out back, but I didn't see him. I'll go out again after the sun comes up."

"I'll check on the beach." Cody walked over to the front entrance which was still blocked by jagged rocks and debris. "Buddy isn't tall enough to reach the opening in the back tunnel. He probably went out right here." Cody looked out through the small opening, then pulled down several more rocks to increase the size of the hole.

With a handgun under his belt, he crawled through, convinced it would not collapse on him.

~ ~ ~

Diamond waited anxiously while Cody went out on his own again. She walked toward the interior section near the shower where she found Parker sitting alone. "Is it okay if I talk to you, Mr. Parker?"

"It's difficult to watch him suffer, isn't it, child?"

She sat down. "How did you know what I wanted to say?"

"You aren't hard to read."

"Mr. Parker, I, uh . . . I don't know how to ask this . . ."

"You want to know why Cody is so moody, right?"

Her troubled eyes gave away her feelings.

"What's your definition of love, Diamond?"

"Love? Uh, finding someone to be with who makes me feel good about myself. That's what I've always thought."

"So, have you ever found anyone who makes you feel that way?"

She could not hide her frown. "Well, I . . ."

"You see, we all have the same vocabulary, but we don't all use the same dictionary, in a manner of speaking."

"Tell me something I can understand. Please."

"Greater love has no man than this, that he would lay down his life for a friend."

"Let me guess. That's from the Bible?"

"When someone is touched by the God who really sees and really hears, uh, someone like Cody for example, it changes one's definitions, especially the meaning of love. True love can sometimes be measured by pain. A heart that loves the most is the one most easily broken."

"Mr. Parker, you're going to make me cry again."

"Real love calls you into someone else's pain. It's love that puts Cody in conflict with evil every day. If he isn't lifting up his hand to the helpless, he's not whole. But that is a difficult road to walk alone. He makes a mistake by not letting someone in."

"Cody used that word *whole* earlier. He said I would be *whole* again. I told him I have never been whole."

Parker's 81-year-old eyes glistened. "You must give your life away to be whole. Exchange your life for the one God has for you."

The hunger in Diamond's voice gave away her feelings. "We got on that plane just four days ago. Who would've ever thought I would be wanting what I want now."

~   ~   ~

The sun was still below the horizon when Cody made his way down the hill toward the water. He favored the sore knee he had bruised the day before while tumbling into the bushes during the gorilla incident. He spotted the tiny figure of a dark-headed boy sitting alone on the beach near the gently-splashing surf. The bodies from the crash and the floating luggage had apparently been washed out to sea. The storm may have taken care of that.

The tail of the commuter aircraft remained tall in the water, like a marker to the departed.

Though the sun had not yet made its appearance, a faint orange hue had begun to fill a spectacular eastern sky. Cody cautiously looked around. His first thought was to scold the boy for running off and jeopardizing the safety of all. But as he approached the child, he instinctively slowed his steps. The serenity was golden.

Everyone has a story to tell. Everyone needs an audience. They were of the same mind — he and this child who had been forced to chase away the shadow of death way too soon. What was his story? Would he ever be able to tell anyone? Would he ever even say a word? The last thing this child needed right now was a lecture.

Cody sat down at Buddy's right side, slowly, silently, so as to not disturb the moment.

"Hello, Gunfighter," the boy said without even looking up. "I'm sorry I make things hard for you. I make things hard for everybody."

Cody, surprised, hesitated before speaking. He sensed that Diamond had followed, that she was now standing behind them keeping her distance.

"You know, son, I prefer 'Cody' instead of 'Gunfighter.' See, Gunfighter is a codename assigned by the people I work with, but Cody is my real name, and that's what my friends call me. What's your name? I mean, if we're gonna be friends, I need to know what to call you."

"Freddy. My name is Freddy Reyes. I am from Colón City in Panama."

"Well, Freddy, why haven't you talked to us before now?"

"Because I am afraid. I am troublemaker. I know your real name is Cody Musket. I heard everyone talking. Why do you want to be my friend, Cody Musket? I never had a friend before because I am big troublemaker."

"Well, I been known as a troublemaker myself. In fact, I been known to need all the friends I can get. A friend is a real gift."

"Is the actor lady your woman? I heard the others talking."

Cody sighed. "Well, see, you gotta be careful about listening to what everybody says. But why do you wanna know if she's my woman?"

Freddy dropped his head again and said nothing.

"I wanna ask you another question, Freddy. Is that okay?"

The boy shrugged his shoulders.

"Why did you hide under that tarp on the boat? Why didn't you get off with the other kids?"

"Because of the pops. I don't like pops."

"Pops?"

"Yes, the pops were the same as when my father . . ."

"What did your father do, son? Can you tell me? I will always be your friend. You can tell me anything."

Freddy began to sob. He placed his head against Cody's ribs, his small body shaking with a memory.

"You don't have to tell me right now, son."

"I am sorry I cry, Cody Musket. I want to be a man, like you."

"Well," Cody said, "the greatest Man who ever lived was named Jesus, and He had friends who wrote about the stuff they saw him do. One of 'em wrote the words, 'Jesus wept.' So, even the strongest men cry sometimes."

Diamond covered her mouth with both hands and fought hard to conceal the sound of her own crying.

"My father shot my mother, and then he shot himself. I was watching from under the bed."

Cody turned his head away. Despite what he had just said, he didn't want Freddy to see the tears welling up in his own eyes. Behind him, he could hear Diamond whispering, *"Oh, God, no."*

"After that, I go to live with my Aunt Linda in Panama City. She said it was my fault my mother and father were dead. She said nobody wants me because I am too much trouble. She sold me to a man with big red truck. He said I go to work in gold mine. No one want me. Nobody listen. I stop talking."

Diamond eased forward and sat beside Freddy on his left.

"Hello, actor lady. Did you hear what I said?"

"Yes, Freddy, I heard." She placed her arm around his shoulders.

Cody searched for words. "Freddy, when people are afraid, they sometimes look for someone else to blame. You have to forgive them."

"Why should I forgive them?"

"Well . . . see, Jesus said that when you forgive somebody it messes with their head."

Freddy frowned. "What does that mean?"

"Uh, okay . . . it means they'll have second thoughts. It might change their whole attitude about stuff, maybe even turn their life around. It'll also set you free from all the hurt you're feeling."

"Cody Musket, who was the other man in the water?"

"The other man? It was just the two of us, Freddy. Nobody else."

"What does Jesus look like? How will I know if I see Him?"

"Well, I think, uh . . . if you ever see Him, you'll know who He is. And don't worry about Jesus. He's been known to choose His best friends from people that nobody else wants, especially troublemakers like us."

"Cody Musket, do you and your woman want me?"

Cody and Diamond exchanged an awkward glance. She nodded.

"So, Freddy, maybe you should call her 'Mama Diamond.' I have the feeling lots of kids will be calling her by that name soon."

Freddy grinned. "So that means you will have lots of babies soon?"

Cody stood and took Freddy's hand. "Don't get ahead of yourself, little guy."

Cody reached for Diamond with his free hand. "We need to head back to the cave before we're spotted. The sun's coming up fast."

He led them up the hill. When they reached the plateau at the top, Freddy asked, "Cody Musket, can I have a codename like you?"

"Like I said, don't be getting ahead of yourself."

"What does that mean?"

Suddenly, a chilling voice rang out from below. *"Detener! No te muevas!"* ("Stop! Don't move!")

Diamond screamed and snatched Freddy into her arms as Cody turned to look. Three armed individuals, one woman and two men, stood at the bottom of the hill with guns raised. The shrill voice was that of the woman.

A large gray-haired man wearing a red bandana around his head stepped forward. He spoke English. "Ha! We been looking for you, amigo. I didn't realize you'd brought the missus and your kid with you to this scenic Caribbean paradise. Yer a long way from home ain't you, boy?"

The man appeared twice Cody's age and would have blended well on main street in Dodge City around 1881. His hair was long enough to wrap around his wide head like a turban, and was held in place by the red bandana headband. His thick spectacles were horn-rimmed, and he wore a rugged version of buckskin from head to toe. He sported two holstered six-guns belted around his waist, a Bowie knife on his hip, and carried an assault weapon in his right hand.

Cody could feel Diamond's fear as she pressed against him still holding Freddy. Cody threw his hands into the air and stepped forward.

"Praise the Lord!" Cody yelled down the hill. "I'm so glad to finally see somebody from home! You must be from, uh, lemme guess . . . Amarillo? See, I'm from Texas, and this here's my woman and kid. We come on 'nis here vacation, you see? And that airplane jes flat took a nose dive on us. So, have you come to rescue us, sir?"

The big man at the bottom of the hill stared at Cody for a moment but said nothing. Finally, he broke the silence. "Hmmm, now just tell me how many survived and where they been holdin' out at, and we jus' might be able to help you out, son."

Freddy's eyes were as big as saucer plates. He whispered, "Cody Musket, he is a gunfighter too. I hope Jesus is watching."

"Cody," Diamond whispered. "Look at the airplane!"

Cody glanced out to sea. The tail of the downed commuter was turning in circles, as if Leviathan, that monster of the deep, were waltzing playfully on the ocean floor holding the hidden parts of the plane in his death grip.

The ground began to shake again. This time, the rumbling could be felt like deep concussions. Cody and Diamond lost their footing and were quickly on the ground. They struggled to keep little Freddy from sliding away. They managed to stay on the plateau next to the cave entrance.

A minute later, the tremors stopped. A rock slide had cleared the hill of most foliage and debris, and there was no sign of the three individuals at the bottom. Victor emerged from the cave. "Anyone injured?"

No one had been hurt. But one glance toward the reef gave new meaning to the term "shock and awe."

The water along the reef bubbled and steamed. The aircraft fuselage and tail were gone.

17

WILD BILL

Victor helped Cody, Diamond, and Freddy return to the cave through the small opening in the rocks. Victor had heard every word of Cody's conversation with the man at the bottom of the hill.

Cody sat down and pulled up the leg of his pants. "This knee's still sore, but I can make it. We need to get outta here. The sooner, the better."

"I agree," Victor said. "But this area is still being patrolled. If we make a run for it now, we'll certainly be intercepted. It will be especially hard with you and Tige injured."

"I already said I can make it."

"Cody, take it easy. Victor's not the enemy." Diamond was afraid she had overstepped. "I mean, I'm just saying —"

"Okay, okay," Cody said. "My knee's still sore, and Tige's leg is still banged up. But we gotta do what we have to do. And we need to get creative."

Victor chuckled. "Creative? I'm just waiting to see what you come up with next. You think Wild Bill bought your vacation act?"

Diamond could not resist. "That wuz purdy special, if ya' ax me. Too bad I ain't have no chaw o' tobacco 'tween my teeth at the time. I shore cudda spit. That wudda convinced 'em."

Cody and Victor were speechless. Even Freddy frowned momentarily.

"I wonder if he wudda recognized Annie Oakley here," Cody said. "It certainly convinced me." He glanced at Diamond.

"No telling," Victor answered. "But since Diamond is one of their targets, he may have recognized her, and there's another problem that's even bigger."

"I know," Cody agreed. "Did you see the plane move?"

"Affirmative. It's freakin' gone. Are you thinkin' what I am?"

Cody exhaled, then looked at Diamond. "This island may be getting ready to explode. I'm not a geologist or seismologist, but there's something pretty freaky about this island — the sulfur smell, the water bubbling, the steam."

Diamond wavered. "What are you guys talking about?"

"This cave was formed by a volcanic eruption. I wonder how long this volcano has been dormant."

Diamond gasped. "We're sitting on a volcano? Is it going to erupt?"

"It happens all the time," Victor said. "This place may have erupted in pre-civilization times. Maybe five thousand years ago, maybe longer."

"So, how long before it erupts again? Is there any way to know?"

Victor scratched his head. "Based on the signs, it could be weeks, could be days. Might not erupt at all."

"But neither of us is a scientist," Cody reminded. "We need to contact the outside world and find out what's going on."

Victor weighed in again. "I'd bet those gorilla whisperers in that compound are aware. Wonder how much they'd stand to lose if this place got vaporized."

"Not to mention, all of us vaporized as well," Diamond said.

"Okay." Cody scratched his chin. "I have an idea. Before we do anything, we need to relocate. We could create a diversion on the east side like we talked about yesterday. Guerrilla tactics, disruptive, make 'em think we've moved into that area. That might draw the hostiles away from this side and give us a chance to move safely to the other cave."

Victor responded. "It's about a three-mile walk to the east side. We'd have to stay within the tree line for cover. It's dangerous, but I don't see us havin' any other choice."

Cody nodded. "Exactly. It won't be long 'till this hiding place gets discovered. We need to clear this area."

"What kind of guerrilla tactics do you have in mind?"

"Like I said earlier, we'll have to get creative. If we can make them think we're holed up somewhere on the east side, we can get everybody relocated and then figure out a way to sneak into the enemy compound while they are all out searching on the wrong side of the island."

Diamond objected. "Cody, there are too many people guarding that compound. You wouldn't stand a chance."

Victor gathered items for the trip to the east side. "Angel said this place is run by three hundred people, but only forty-five are armed and trained for combat."

Betsy joined them. "That's too many against too few."

"Also, Cody, think about this." Diamond crossed her arms. "Before you go charging into that compound, shouldn't you interrogate the prisoners to find out what they know?"

Victor grinned. "That's smart thinking. If those guys in the hole knew about the possible volcano eruption, they might be willing to talk."

"Okay." Cody nodded again. "We'll question them when we get back. Our objectives are to save the kids and get outta here. The possible eruption might take care of putting this place out of existence, but we gotta save the kids first."

"That's right," Tige finally spoke up. "There's kids in that compound, and if this place explodes, those cold-blooded killers won't stop to help the children."

As the two men prepared to leave for their guerrilla mission on the east side of the island, Diamond pulled Cody to the side. "You come back to me, Cody Musket. I . . . that is *we* . . . we need you." She kissed him.

Cody answered with only a grimacing smile.

"I know, Gunfighter, I know." She put her hand over Cody's lips. "Don't say anything. Right now, you . . . I mean *we* . . . have a mission."

Victor and Cody squeezed through the exit hole then hastened their steps, being watchful and careful to stay covered by the brush near the shoreline. After a three-hour walk, they sat down in a secluded spot to listen. They heard voices in the distance.

Victor whispered, "So what now, genius? You gonna come up with another gorilla sighting?"

"Stay here," Cody said under his breath. "I'm goin' closer. I wanna determine how many people are out there."

Cody moved cautiously toward the voices but could not see anyone. He stopped and hid in a trough covered by a fallen tree limb. He listened.

"Well, hello again, pilgrim!"

Cody looked up. He had been taken completely by surprise. Standing before him was the massive individual with the rough buckskins who had stood at the bottom of the hill that morning. He looked much larger up close.

"Somethin' tells me you ain't here on no vacation, son."

"No need to pretend, Wild Bill. We both know this island is ready to explode."

"So then, why are you here? This is an animal research center. Off-limits to the likes o' you. We just want that woman o' yours. She'll go with us. We offer her a way of escape, which is more than you can offer."

"Animal research center? That's strange. I thought the animals were the ones in charge of this place."

"Yer absolutely right, son. And you don't wanna mess with the animals in 'nis fine institution. If you don't hand over the woman, she'll die along with you, and that would be a shame."

"What about the children? I suppose you'll take them with you too?"

"Children? Ha! If I should see any children, I'll let you know. See, we got lotsa assets, like technology that'll change the world. That's what needs savin'. If there was any other assets, as you say, they'd prolly be 'bout used up by now, so we would just pick up a fresh batch of assets. When disaster strikes it's every man for himself, wouldn't you say?"

"If I see a *man* around here," Cody said, "I'll let you know."

Wild Bill snarled. "I just figgered somethin' out. I bet you's the one that stole our assets that come in by boat the other night. But it don't matter now, 'cuz we'd just have to leave them here too."

Cody ground his teeth and stared.

"Now, I know exactly what yer thinkin' about, son. You're thinkin' we have ourselves a good ol' Mexican standoff."

"Not at all, Wild Bill. See, I'm thinkin' that you have assets I want, and I have assets you can't have. I figger I got the advantage."

"Now, let me tell you how this is gonna go, boy. On a count o' three, I'm gonna draw this here Vintage Buntline and blow you straight through the gates o' hell. Unless o' course you can outdraw me with that Glock you're carryin' on your hip."

"Nice try, Bill. I don't have much use for handguns."

"Wait a minute. You saw the movie too?"

"Movie? What movie is that?"

"You know. The one called somethin' down under? Where the guy says he don't have no use for handguns but shoots him anyway?"

"Doesn't matter," Cody replied. "I'm the slowest draw in the west. Besides that, you have a sniper on me, and I have a sniper on you. If anybody draws, we both die. If I die, I go to Heaven and you don't get to find out where my assets are, so I still have the advantage."

Wild Bill wasn't impressed. He spoke slowly, deliberately. "On the count of three, pilgrim. One . . . two . . ." Suddenly, his face was as pale as the *Headless Horseman*. His mouth flew open, his gray-wolf eyes focused on something above Cody's head. *"Gorilla! Gorilla!"*

Cody felt hot air breathing down his neck. He turned to see a gorilla the size of Vesuvius staring him in the face. Its growl made the earth shake. Its fists sounded like the Guns of Navarone beating on the front of its gargantuan chest. Cody dove back into the trees like a mouse escaping the tomcat. At least twenty hunters appeared out of nowhere carrying tranquilizer rifles. The hunt was on.

Cody raced unnoticed back to Victor's hiding place. He was short of breath when he got there. "C'mon! Let's get outta here!"

They hiked their way out of the trees and decided to jog home on the beach. It would be twice as fast as scuffling through the trees again. The troops were busy chasing Godzilla the Third and right now that was their biggest priority. Judging by the triumphant snorting and growling and the certifiably frenzied yelling of the hunters, Godzilla was holding his own.

The late afternoon sun was low in the western sky when Cody and Victor finally returned from the eastern side of the island. They had not eaten all day. As they munched on leftover fruit, Victor shared their brand-new gorilla story. He was a good storyteller and it seemed to lighten everyone's spirits. Freddy sat on Cody's lap.

They decided to sleep for a few hours and then rise at midnight and move their base to the new cave. Their flares were fully charged. They hoped to have an uneventful night transitioning to the new location.

18

FAMILY?

Cody and Victor reveled in the success of their guerrilla incursion. Not only had Godzilla drawn a crowd, but now Wild Bill and company could only guess where Cody and the rest of the survivors were holed up. East? West? In between?

How many of the forty-five armed combatants would be dispatched to the east side, especially if the gorilla managed to evade capture for a couple more days? Would it be enough of a diversion for Cody and Victor to encroach upon the compound and rescue the kids? After that, how would they get off the island before an earthquake or volcano destroyed one and all?

As the group departed their hideout, the night sky was overcast. A mist was falling. Victor took the lead since he knew the way. He also led the four prisoners bound with ropes. Cody followed behind them, still carrying the Glock on his right hip. Behind him, Diamond carried little Freddy, who had fallen back to sleep. Betsy walked beside Tige, who still limped slightly.

Parker was curious. "Ms. Casper, have you or Cody asked Freddy his age?"

"He's five, so he says, but he isn't sure. No one has ever given him a birthday party," she said. "He doesn't even know his birth date."

"He is a blessed child," Parker said. "Have you decided what you'll do with him when we get to the new hideout? Will he stay with you and Cody, or will he stay with the kids? Where will he sleep?"

Cody dropped back a step and walked beside Diamond. "I have an idea," he said. "Why can't you, Freddy, and I sleep with all the kids?"

"All those kids?" Her mouth gaped open. "You mean like one big . . ."

"Family?" Parker asked.

"I wouldn't know. Family's something I never had."

"I remind both of you that I'm still a minister of the gospel," Parker said, chuckling.

Cody and Diamond exchanged glances again. "Well," Cody said, "time will tell. We'll let you know if we, uh, ever need anything."

Diamond swallowed her grin as she handed Freddy to Cody. "Whew, he's getting heavy."

"We've been here four days, but it's hard to count when the nights and days seem the same."

"Right," Tige said. "Especially when we're cooped up in that cave all day."

"We're getting off this island," Cody promised. "We may have the opportunity to get into that compound sooner rather than later. We just need more intel from Angel."

~   ~   ~

When they walked safely into the cave above the cove, Angel was missing. Pablo told them Angel had been taken and locked up. But

Pablo already had a layout of the compound. He also said that thirty-two of the forty-five armed personnel would leave at dawn to look again for the gorilla and the survivors. The search had shifted to the east side.

"Yes!" Cody bumped fists with Victor. "That means our ploy worked! Tomorrow we leave for the compound. We'll free Angel. We'll get those kids and find a way off this island."

Victor had a question for Pablo. "Amigo, are you sure La Luz doesn't suspect you? What if they're feeding you false intel and setting a trap for us? How do you know Angel hasn't cracked under interrogation?"

"I promise you," Pablo said, "Angel would die before giving you up. His two nephews were taken six years ago. He was not able to save them. He didn't tell you. He never talks about it. But . . ." Pablo wiped perspiration from his brow with his sleeve. "We are all committed. Better we die than one of these little ones. Many of them have already suffered too much."

Victor and Cody had a powwow. They agreed that they would invade the compound themselves — just the two of them. They did not want to involve any of Pablo's associates and blow their cover.

Cody and Diamond walked to the area where the children were sleeping. Bedding was crude. The men had brought straw and palm leaves for cushioning against the rock floor and had placed blankets over them. The kids were restless. Many were awake, crying. Some were crawling over other children to find a more comfortable place. Few were asleep.

They made their bed a few feet away from the kids and closed their eyes. "Long day tomorrow," Cody said. "We can still catch a few winks before morning. I'm gonna tell the prisoners about the volcano. It's their lives at stake too. If they want to live, they'll cooperate."

She opened her eyes and turned toward him. Freddy's sleepy head rested on Cody's shoulder. "Cody, there's something I need to say. You don't need to open your eyes. Just listen, okay?"

Just then she was startled to feel something push against her foot. She looked down to see a child about Freddy's size placing himself next to her ankles. In minutes, she and Cody were surrounded by small, frail children migrating toward the security of two adult humans with warm bodies who spoke kindly to each other. The murmuring and sobbing noises faded.

Cody and Diamond found each other's eyes. "Cody, I have never . . . I could never get used to this."

"No one should ever have to see what you're seeing right now. This is what love starvation looks like. Summa' these kids are never held or touched by a loving adult."

"Cody, a week ago, I would never have believed that a moment like this could happen to me."

"Doesn't surprise me."

"Nothing surprises you. How can you be so old at just twenty-two?"

"I've seen this before, but only once." Cody sighed while Freddy positioned himself directly between them. "My family has battled child slavery for almost three decades. Our resources are almost used up."

"Resources?"

"Yeah, it gets harder and harder to raise money. The Musket fortune is nearly gone. But I have a plan — the pirate treasure."

"Pirate treasure? In the cave? But, how?"

"It's a secret. Trust me, you're safer not knowing."

"Okay, I won't ask."

"This is 2041," he said. "You'd think that by now we would have driven the trafficking evil off the planet. One day the world will be free."

"Is that what keeps you going?"

"No. You wanna know what keeps me going? The little eyes that can only stare into empty space. Tiny fingers . . . 'specially the ones that've never even experienced a handshake. Thin little arms that . . . that would come alive if somebody, just any caring person, would offer a hug. Yeah, that's what keeps me in this game."

"Game? I can see you're a sad person, Cody. I've never cried in my life unless men were hurting me. I never knew there were so many other reasons in this world to shed tears."

"I have a confession," Cody said. "I want to kiss you right now, but since we have Freddy between us it would be a difficult maneuver."

"*Maneuver?*" She grinned. "So, maybe you need to develop a different *tactical approach* for kissing when someone is in the way."

"Like I said before, you have a way with words."

She brushed back her hair. "Cody, I've never had a real life. The films I've made, the people I've charmed to get ahead — my whole life built on make-believe. Now, it's my time to say something real."

"I'm all ears." Cody leaned his head on one elbow. "I wasn't planning to sleep anyway."

She answered with a dry chuckle. "Okay, here goes." She covered her face again. "Oh, I'm going to cry. I hate that." She wiped her face and strengthened her resolve. "So . . . Cody, I'm like some of these kids, the ones starved for a touch of . . . of love. I never knew I could be loved until these last few days. Do you remember when I told you I could never let a man touch me again? I mean, you remember, right?"

"I'm listening."

"So, you said the day would come that I'd be whole."

"Hmmm, go ahead. I remember."

"So, it's like this, see, I've never *chosen* to be with any man. I was always forced. But, right now . . . I mean, I've *never* felt this way."

"I knew it would happen," Cody said. "Eventually, that is."

"So, Mr. Parker made us an offer in case we ever . . ." She shut her heavy eyelids. "*Ohhh,* I can't stop these tears. Something about this place."

Cody reached for her hand. "Okay. You start working on your cryin' and I'll brush up on my tactical approach. By the time we get off this island, we should both have our acts together."

"You have your own way with words, Mr. Musket. I never know when you're kidding."

"Seriously." He shut his eyes and squeezed her hand. "Don't be ashamed of your tears. You've earned them all."

19

BETRAYAL

Cody and Diamond arose at dawn. Neither had slept soundly. Today was mission day. The children who had surrounded them while they slept were beginning to stir. When Cody tried to raise himself off the floor, Freddy clung to him. The child seemed to know something was up.

"Cody Musket, will you leave again? Mama Diamond cried when you were gone yesterday. Everyone said it was dangerous. When you came back I was happy. I heard the talking last night. You will leave again today?"

Cody struggled. How do you explain to a child that the island is going to explode and become uninhabitable? How can you tell a five-year-old that you have no idea what to expect when you get to the compound? Would he and Victor be able to find the child workers in time undetected and free them? And even if they were successful, would they be able to escape the island?

He did his best to assure the child, but had to tear himself away, leaving Freddy in tears.

He met with Pablo again and devised a plan to enter the compound on the bottom floor. Thirty-two of the forty-five armed personnel would supposedly be deployed at dawn to the east side once more, leaving only thirteen combatants to defend the compound. Pablo said he would leave early to make certain there would be no surprises.

After Pablo departed, Cody heard something he did not want to hear.

"I spoke to the prisoners a few minutes ago," Victor said. "One was ready to talk. He claims he was brought here against his will."

"You believe him?"

"It was worth a try. I told the prisoners about the volcano. The others laughed it off, but this guy wanted to help. I've been doing this a while. He doesn't seem hardened like the other three you captured."

"So, did he give you anything Pablo hadn't told us?'

Victor frowned and drew a deep breath. Cody knew something was wrong.

"He says his real name is Casey Scott." Victor began reading from his interrogation notes. "American former black ops. Specialist in chemical warfare and advanced tactical electronics. Graduate of JFK Special Warfare Center. Served with the 160th Spec. Ops Airborne. Engineering degrees from Cambridge and MIT. Thirty-five years of age. Claims his own thirteen-year-old boy was kidnapped and brought here. That's how they 'recruited' him. He's being forced to develop weapons of mass destruction here. And something else . . . I'll let him tell you."

Victor brought the prisoner forward.

"So, Mr. Scott. I understand you have information for us. Call me *Gunfighter*. And remember, I didn't get the codename accidentally."

"I understand, sir. I must first warn you. Pablo is not on your side."

"Prove it."

"I've been informed that he's turned. I've been out of pocket since I was captured, but Carter told me it was a pre-arrangement. I'm certain that he's prepared a surprise party for you guys. If you take me with you, I can show you where they'll probably set up an ambush. My son Joshua is just thirteen. He was kidnapped and brought here. That's how they forced me to develop WMDs for 'em. They said if I ever wanted to see him in one piece again . . . I mean, you know the drill. Joshua's all I have. I panicked. I betrayed my country and all the children of the world to save my son. I was a fool." He swallowed hard. Cody gave him a bottle of water.

"I mostly do R&D, but I double as a scout from time to time. That's what I was doing when you caught us. You're pretty good. My head didn't stop ringing for a whole day."

"Why didn't you try to contact the outside world long ago? I mean, if you're as brilliant as you say, why didn't you try to do something?"

"They keep us in small cubicles. We work, then we go back to those tiny holes under lock and key. The *Sabonic Cage Umbrella* prevents all communications from leaving or arriving here, and does not allow overhead surveillance of the island, even from satellites. The rest of the world doesn't even know this place exists."

"Sabonic Cage Umbrella? What's that?"

"That's the overhead shield. When La Luz wants to reach points outside the shield, they take a boat beyond the barrier reef and call out. The shield is a super Esper-Wave light bender. Makes the blue Caribbean Sea appear to go right through this area. Makes the island invisible from above."

Cody and Victor looked at each other.

"Look," Scott said. "If this island is going up in smoke, we're all gonna die anyway. I'll surrender to authorities as soon as we get outta here, but I wanna stop these guys more than you. My son doesn't receive enough to eat, or get medical help. The work isn't physically difficult, but the conditions are horrible and . . . Please, sir. Let me help you."

Cody and Victor signaled thumbs-up to each other, deciding to place their trust with Casey Scott.

"Give this man another water bottle," Cody said. "Give him his boots and britches. We're going to war."

The three men made their way toward the compound. Scott brought them to a halt at a location about a half mile from the main entrance of the tall structure which was built on the side of the mountain. The volcano crater was at the top of said mountain.

"Take a look thirty degrees off center," Scott said. "What do you see?"

Victor gazed through the field glasses and counted. "I see two, four, five, seven, uh, eleven tangos in the trees. More may be hidden. I see eight to the left. Distance about a hundred meters."

"That adds up to nineteen against three," Cody said. "Those aren't good odds," We'll never even reach the entry. Got any ideas?"

"Follow me," Scott said. "I'll take you in through a door they won't expect. No one is supposed to know about this, but I figured it out within my first four days."

Scott was lean and fast despite having been held captive several days. With an evening shadow on his scowling face, urgent eyes, and an *Airborne* tat on his forearm, he appeared to be all he claimed. Cody and Victor had no choice but to place their bets on him. As they made their way toward a secret entry, the terrain became steeper and steeper. They moved parallel to a rock fence that served as a security barrier for the compound. Halfway up, Scott halted again and began digging. He uncovered a two-foot-square electrical box, then opened the top and punched several buttons.

"Now," Scott said, catching his breath after the uphill jog. "We wait sixty seconds for the system to reboot. A door will become visible on the rock barrier."

Victor was also panting. "Okay." He swiveled his head in every direction. "No one following so far."

"That's because they're all waiting back on the main road," Scott said. "They don't know I'm with you."

Cody sat down to slow his breathing. "Where you from, Scott?"

"Marysville, California. Not far from the old Beale Air Force Base where they once based the SR-71 Blackbird. Even though the bird is only a museum piece now, I was always fascinated by how that aircraft was developed before its time. I was never interested in flying. It was always about the technology with me."

"Why didn't you approach me about your situation when I captured you. Why wait 'til now?"

"No offense, Gunfighter, but I didn't figure you had a chance to survive. You may have outsmarted me by faking that rock slide, but you would never want to go up against me again. I wasn't about to trust you. You're just a kid. I figured it would cost my son his life if I revealed anything to you."

"You almost waited too late," Cody said. "Now, here we are."

"Like I said," Scott breathed. "The volcano changes the game. Besides, I might've been wrong about you, Gunfighter. It seems you've turned La Luz on its ear the last few days. I gotta trust somebody before it's too late."

Cody nodded. "Ain't that the truth," he agreed.

At that moment, an oval-shaped pattern appeared on the rock wall. It was transparent, like a partially-developed photo.

"Let's go, gentlemen." Scott led them toward the image, which now resembled an oval flag blowing in the breeze. The flag image became a large hole, then a tunnel which looked much like a natural cave.

They followed Scott into the tunnel. The hole closed behind them. Darkness gave way to an amber-lighted passage which led to another oval opening in a metal barrier.

They passed through the barrier. "We're in," Scott said. "Look behind you."

When Cody and Victor looked back, the passage behind them was now crisscrossed with amber laser beams. "Obviously, you can't come back this way, gentlemen."

"Here," Cody said, handing Scott a Glock 17 handgun and a CT 4780 laser assault rifle. "I have a feeling you know how to use these."

They moved ahead into a dimly-lit hallway with windows spaced evenly along both sides. "This is where they kept us — the R&D specialists," Scott said. "Cubicles. Comfortable, but small and lonely. My cell is number 00890."

They walked cautiously, glancing into each window along the way. It was gruesome. Every cell contained a lifeless body, a corpse.

"They must have gassed them all," Scott said. "We all knew it would happen someday. They had no plans for us to leave the island. We knew too much. I guess they considered this a humane way for them to die, as opposed to burning alive in molten lava. I would've been dead with them if you hadn't captured me. I suppose I should thank you."

They moved a little farther and came to Scott's cell. Scott looked inside, expecting it to be empty. But it wasn't.

Scott caught Cody by the arm. "Take a look inside."

Cody moved to the window, then beat his fist against the glass. Victor took a look.

"He was a good man," Victor said. "I guess we know what happened to Angel now. Pablo probably took care of that too."

"What about the kids?" Cody said. "Let's keep moving."

"The kids?" Scott bristled. "Right this way, Gunfighter. But I'm afraid of what I'm gonna find."

He took Cody and Victor through a door into a large expanse. The sides of the cavern sparkled with gold flakes. A bubbling underground river ran until it stretched beyond range of the limited light. It was misty, dark, cryptic. They heard a low mumble. As they moved forward, the child barracks came into view.

Concrete walls about six feet in height, steel bars in modest windows. A look inside revealed bunks, showers, toilets, a few tables, and about sixty weary, traumatized children. Most appeared to be teenagers, some younger. Boys and girls were separated by a wall.

"They're alive!" Scott whispered. "Joshua! Josh?" He got no response.

The murmuring began to swell. The hands of children began reaching through the bars. Cody sank to one knee. "How do we get them out? How do we get them out?? Do you hear me??" He turned his head toward Scott who was entering the code to open the doors.

"It doesn't work!" Scott lamented quietly. "They changed the code! *Dammit!* They knew we were coming. They won't let these kids go even now because they know too much, just like us."

"Scott! Get a hold on yourself," Victor said. "How do we get the new code?"

Scott cleared his mind with a deep breath. "Okay, we have to move. They will be on to us. We gotta go up two floors and enter the central control area. Look there for a panel marked *GK-Niner-Niner-14.*"

Cody and Victor exchanged nods. Cody then glanced at Scott. "Lead the way, Army! This is your command."

As they were leaving, Victor turned his head and spoke loudly in Spanish to the children, asking them to not abandon hope.

They climbed two sets of stairs and walked into another hallway with offices on either side. Several of the bullet-proof sliding doors were open. The lighting was dim, but brighter than below.

When they reached the end of the hall, they came to a security door. An adult male voice was shouting orders on the other side. Cody and Victor braced themselves.

Suddenly, something like a cannonball struck Cody in the abdomen. A force drove him sideways and wrestled him to the floor. Before Cody could even blink, Victor landed beside him. They heard a door slide shut. Cody and Victor were locked inside one of the rooms.

As Cody tried to recover the breath that had been knocked from him, someone was speaking.

"Gentlemen, listen carefully. This door will automatically open in fifty seconds. Turn left, left again, then turn right, walk thirty paces, and enter the control center. Gunfighter, I slipped the entry code into your pocket. Free those kids. Find my boy. He's only thirteen. He . . . he likes to be called 'Josh.' You guys can't die, that's an order."

Cody and Victor pounded on the door, but it was no use. A gun battle ensued in the hallway. Shouting, shooting, men falling. In a moment, it was over. Forty seconds had passed. The remaining ten seconds seemed like a silent eternity.

The sliding door opened right on schedule. Spent gunpowder smoke clouded the hallway, but it could not hide the blunt truth — six dead tangos, one dead former Army Ranger with a son who liked to be called 'Josh.'

Victor spoke with reverent tone. "C'mon Gunfighter. Army cleared the way. Let's make it count."

The two men moved through the door, which had come at a steep price. They followed Scott's instructions and came to the control center. The entry door was eight feet across and made of bullet-proof, transparent steel glass. Cody felt in his front pocket and found a handwritten note with an entry code as promised. He opened the door.

The room was laid out like the bridge of a super ocean-going vessel. Consecutive bay windows formed the curvature of the front wall and overlooked the shining Caribbean Sea. A narrow, turning stairway rose to an outside observatory. The multifunctional display panels were intimidating — radar overlays, weather charts, con screens, rapid rotation code numbers, security systems, polished burl conference table, and more.

As they looked through the windows, they discovered a frightening reality. The volcano crater at the top of the mountain was smoking. Dark gray ash clouded the air. An eruption could be imminent.

"We need to expedite." Victor's voice sharp, thin. "We have only minutes 'til more armed personnel will be at that door."

"If I have an entry code," Cody said, "somebody else does too."

"Look for that panel Scott told us about. The one programmed to open that dungeon downstairs. We also gotta find a way to get the kids back to our hideout without getting caught."

"Yeah," Victor said. "Then we have to find a way to get 'em off the island before that hill decides to blow. By the way, here comes our reception party."

Cody turned to look. Seven more armed soldiers were attempting to enter the room through the transparent steel door. They were unable. Scott may have changed the code remotely before giving him the entry digits. But how would he have had time? One thing seemed certain: That door was the only visible means of departure. They would have to get past the seven who would be waiting for them outside the door.

At that moment, they felt another tremor. They looked toward the mountain. Several darker billows of smoke were rising into the air. Then, something else caught their attention. In the opposite corner of the room, two young girls lay motionless on the floor. They were blond, perhaps early teens.

"Wonder if they're alive," Cody said. "They don't look like the other kids. Better dressed, not so depleted."

"I know one way to find out." Victor started toward the girls, then was knocked to the floor by the worst tremor yet. Everything in the room rattled for about three minutes.

As the two men picked themselves up, they noticed that the glass door area was now clear. The tangos had fled.

Victor started toward the two girls again, but halted when he and Cody simultaneously caught sight of a large man coming down the circular stairway from the observatory above. The big man looked familiar. When he reached floor level, he came and stood facing them.

"Seems like we just keep meetin' up, don't it, pilgrim? Must mean we are destined to find our fate at each other's hand."

"Hello, Wild Bill. Looks like all your help is leaving. It's a shame they've deserted you at a time like this."

"Look, Cody, I have what you want. I'm gonna toss it to your friend here. It's the code to release the kids in the bunker downstairs. You'll also find a back door to a tunnel that leads directly to four boats. Now, them paddle-skippers only hold about eight people each, but you're welcome to squeeze as many o' them sixty kids on as you can."

He tossed the code to Victor, who looked at Cody. Cody motioned him to leave and get the kids to safety.

"So you learned my name?" Cody said. "I'm impressed with your generosity. Thanks for the boats."

"Not so fast, Musket. It's too bad you won't be able to get yourself and your lady friend on board unless you throw off some o' them kids. And what about my other twenty-four kids you got holed up in the cove? Too many people. Not enough boats. Which ones live? Which ones die?"

"So you know about the cove and the other cave? Doesn't surprise me since Pablo's workin' for you. So why didn't you just take the kids and wipe us out?"

"We was gonna do that, but the volcano makes it irrelevant.

You and most of them kids will die anyway. There is no way off this island."

"So, let me guess; I get more boats if I do what? Fight you to the death?"

"There are no more boats, son. That's it. We had another landing craft on the way, but pirates stole it yesterday. It's headed to Caracas. I got no more boats. Them old landing craft is rare, and we're so far from everywhere no one can get here on time. None of my contacts with helicopters will chance it with the mountain getting' ready to blow."

"Somehow, I don't believe you," Cody said. "You're just playin' games."

"You see, son, it's time for us to complete our destiny. I see you're still wearin' the Glock."

"I told you I didn't have much use for handguns."

"Well, I shudda been born in the 1800s. I was born in the wrong century. Get ready on the count of three."

"Well," Cody said, "this ain't Dodge City and you ain't, uh, Clint Eastwood."

The old man's eyes lit up like ball lightning. His face was wild and crazed. Cody knew he was going to draw.

"One . . . Two . . . Three!"

"Cody pulled his Glock and fired two shots left of center chest. The old man coughed, staggered, and fell to the floor.

Cody stood over him. The old man had never even drawn his Buntline.

"You . . . you lied to me, son. You did see the movie. I shudda known. But you got the name wrong. It was Wyatt Earp, *not Clint Wassisname.*"

"Stupid ol' man, why didn't you draw?"

"I didn't want to kill you, Cody. This world needs ornery young hombres like you. Men who won't settle. That's the thing about me, all my people are settlers. Like the guys who ran from this door and took off with one of my boats a few minutes ago. Like that Pablo, always crowin' about some pirate treasure rumored to be some place on this island. But it's guys like that what's made me so successful."

"Successful? Who are you anyway?"

"Name's Cupertino. Welcome to my world."

"*You're* Cupertino? The billionaire with a worldwide empire? Why were you even here? Even with the goldmine, this little island's hardly worth your time."

"Well, see, this island was the fun part. I hid from the world, developed next-level gadgets, and helped get hundreds of kids off the street."

"Kids off the street? So then, what we saw downstairs a few minutes ago; that was you doin' a good deed?"

"Look, you did me a favor today, boy. See, I had only six months to live. I got a brain tumor makin' me do crazy stuff. I could've out-drawn you easy. You're fast. They didn't give you the codename 'Gunfighter' for nothing. But I'm faster. Ida' killed you sure. But I had a plan. I went out on my own terms. That's what I call success."

"You're dyin' on the wrong side of the fight, old man. I don't call that success."

"Now, Cody, you're ruinin' my good feeling about how I'm going out. Success? *Ha!* You wanna know how much I've accumulated? How much I'm leavin' behind?"

"All of it," Cody said. "You're leavin' all of it. You've built your life on the backs of child laborers and men who settle for second best. Now, you have nothing left except an island that's about to bury itself. You have only minutes live, and you have no idea what's waiting for you. What's there to feel good about?"

"*Ha!* Jesus? Joe Parker tried that on me and it doesn't work. I actually tried being religious once, and I never became the new person he said I would become."

"Have you ever tried Jesus Himself?"

"You actually think He'd listen to the likes of me?"

"How long do you think you'd last if you had to endure what He did? He suffered to pay for every evil thought you've ever had. He only wants you to trust Him."

"I never trusted nobody." Cupertino coughed up blood. "Ain't gonna begin now."

"Well, sir, you've got about a minute to live. Seems like a good time to start."

"You don't give up do you? Look, Cody, take my key and my card."

"What's this?" Cody examined Cupertino's access card.

"The key to my Beaver and the code to the airplane hangar on the beach behind us. I was planning to escape in the plane, but you saw to it I wouldn't. You're gonna need to get your woman outta here and those two girls that's playin' dead back there."

Suddenly, the two girls on the floor jumped up. One shouted, "How did you know??" She was bouncy and athletic with shifty blue eyes, wavy blond hair, and an apparent flair for drama.

Cody leaped at least a foot off the floor. "Why were you girls playin' dead?"

The bubbly vocal one replied. "Why? Because it worked just fine in Spider-Man 17. And, FYI, you both got the name wrong. It was Doc Holliday, not Wyatt Earp or Clint Eastwood! I'm Kennedy and this is my sister Maggie."

"You saw the movie?" Cupertino wanted to know.

The girls stepped forward then stopped abruptly. Seeing Cupertino on the floor with blood flowing from bullet wounds in his chest shocked them both. Suddenly, this wasn't make-believe.

"The movie? It was . . . it was *Quigley Down Under.*" Kennedy put both hands over her mouth. Her voice trailed off to a whisper. "We thought you guys were just . . . just shinin' around."

"Take this card and this here key, Cody. Get moving. I don't want yawl to . . . to see me . . . die."

"Mr. Cupertino, is there a cell or sat phone around here?"

Cupertino didn't respond. He was gone.

Maggie, the previously silent one, spoke up. "I have a cell phone, the replicent neutronium type." She brushed back her long, straight hair.

"I have one too," Kennedy said. "Maggie stole the phones."

"Lemme see that phone, Maggie."

"Here you are, Mr. Musket. I stole two of these so Kennedy could have one too. I reprogrammed several secure areas in this building and ran a corbo-mydium sweep using their own compuribion electronics to locate hidden phones." She shifted her weight nervously. "So, would you like me to find one for you?"

"Uh, it won't be necessary, Maggie. There isn't time to search for another phone. May I borrow yours?"

Maggie's sky-blue eyes glistened with tears. She couldn't take her eyes off the dead body on the floor. "Of course. This phone isn't really mine, anyway."

"So, you girls were gonna try to call your mom?"

"Not exactly. I mean, we were going to order pizza. Kennedy

likes black olives, but . . . ."

"C'mon, girls, we need to expedite."

Kennedy frowned. "Where are we going?"

"We're going on an airplane ride." He led them out the door.

"*Ohhh!*" Maggie's mouth fell open. "Our momma will be mad. She doesn't like us to fly. Not at all! She's afraid of flying."

"Yeah," Kennedy said. "We can't tell our mom about this."

"Why are you girls here? What's your story?" They began running down a flight of stairs.

Maggie, trim and petite, began to breathe faster. "We . . . we stole our mom's car and couldn't find our way back home."

"We kinda got lost," Kennedy blurted.

"So, you stole your mom's car? Now, you're worried because she doesn't want you to fly?"

"Well, mister, you're getting it mixed up. See, we sorta ran out of gas, and we ended up here. We escaped the day we arrived. It was Maggie's idea." The color returned to Kennedy's cheeks.

"Yeah," Maggie said. "We kept near the food and electronics. We stayed a step ahead of them cuz Kennedy set up a Sakdov shifter singularity interference in their security platform."

Kennedy sighed. "Oh, *yes.* I'm *such* a genius. I'm also the cutest girl-geek on this planet."

"Is that a fact? So, how old are you girls?"

"I'm fourteen, Maggie's fifteen. We're from Topeka."

"Kansas?"

"Of course, doh-doh head! Where do you *think* Topeka is?"

They finally reached the bottom of the stairs.

"So, you stole a car and ended up here? You girls need to work on your story."

"So, mister, why is there so much smoke in the air?"

20

THE BEAVER

Cody and the two girls ran down a long set of stairs toward the beach. It seemed never-ending until they made a right curve and saw a metal hangar sitting next to the water. They arrived out of breath. Cody opened the large sliding doors.

"Mr. Musket, why did we have to run so fast?" Maggie asked. "My side's hurting."

"How old did you say you girls were again?"

Kennedy and Maggie looked at each other. "Okay, okay," Kennedy said, "I'm only twelve and Maggie's thirteen. But I'm taller than she is."

Maggie bristled up. "Well!" she said to her sister. "Maybe so, but I'm smarter than you are!"

"You are not! *I'm* the one who—"

"Kennedy! Maggie! Listen to me!" Cody paused to catch his breath. "You see that mountain over there? Do you see the smoke coming out of the top?? That's a volcano. It's gonna blow, and it's gonna do it soon!"

"You mean like Saint Helens or . . . or—"

"That's right! Now listen, ladies. I need your help. I need you to put some of your electronics knowledge to work. A lotta lives depend on what we're about to do. Don't think of yourselves as girls anymore. Think of yourselves as adults from this day forward, okay?"

Both girls stood staring for a moment. Maggie's tears welled up again and Kennedy frowned, but they both snapped out of it.

"Okay, cowboy . . . I mean, Mr. Musket. My friends call me Ken, by the way."

"Of course we'll help, Mr. Musket." Maggie walked toward the aircraft and began to read the data plate on the side of the fuselage.

"What kind of plane is this?" Ken asked.

Maggie had the answer. "This is a DHC-2 Mk1 Turbo Beaver, Converted in 2008. The serial number is—"

"Okay, okay," Cody said. "Thank you, Maggie."

"I was reading it off the data plate on the side of the plane."

"I know, I know. Let's get on board."

"Where do you want us to sit?" Maggie wanted to know.

"I want Ken in the front with me and you in the back."

"So, why—"

"Don't ask. I have my reasons for the seating arrangement. Adults, remember?"

"Yes, sir."

"You need to wear headsets. We can communicate easier."

The headsets were already installed in the aircraft. He showed the girls how to wear them.

Cody started the turbine engine and propelled the amphibious Beaver gently into the water. He then applied full thrust, sending them bouncing over the late-morning surf. He pulled back on the yoke and they were airborne.

"Try not to turn too much," Maggie said. "I get airsick."

"Gonna have to suck it up this time."

"Yuck!"

"No, no," Cody assured. "Just an expression."

Cody flew low, following the north coastline until he spotted the four boats of kids Victor was leading to the cove on the west side of the island. Some of the healthier kids were rowing.

From the air, Cody estimated the island to be about five miles long from east to west and four miles north to south — a very small island with a two-thousand-foot peak in the middle. The volcano crater at the top of the peak was emitting darker and darker smoke.

"Ladies, we're gonna fly over a cove in a couple of minutes. I need the exact lat-long at the mouth of that cove. Get your pocsats ready. Maggie, when I say three, two, one, *mark,* I want you to record the lat-long. Text those coordinates to Ken and she'll enter it into the global positioning system on the panel up here in front, okay?"

"Okay!"

Cody continued following the coast around to the west side. Soon they were approaching the cove. "Maggie, get ready. Three, two, one, *mark.*"

"Got it! Texting to Ken."

"Outstanding. You're doing great!"

"I didn't receive the text! I didn't get it!" Kennedy shouted.

"Okay, okay. The reason you didn't receive it might be due to the Sabonic Cage Umbrella. It interrupts communications. I'm gonna climb above it and see what happens, but first I need to record one more lat-long at a different location."

Cody continued following the coastline around to the other side of the island until he spotted the front entrance to the original cave which they had abandoned. He turned slightly to fly directly over the cave.

"Stand by, Maggie. Three, two, one, *mark*."

"Got it!" she yelled.

Cody throttled up to full power and climbed until the island disappeared from view. He leveled off at 10,000 feet.

"Hey, where did the island go?" Kennedy was frantic. "It's not there anymore!"

"It's still there," Cody explained. "The Sabonic technology not only blocks communications, but it bends the light and makes the area appear to be solid ocean from overhead."

"How cool!" Maggie said.

"Try to text those coordinates now, Maggie."

"Okay . . . done!"

"Uh, I received them," Kennedy said. "But I can't upload them to your panel. Let me check your system." Kennedy read the data tag on the bottom edge of the unit face, then spoke to Maggie. "This unit has a metra-dupic insulator with a countdown shield. It isn't compatible with these pocsats you lifted from the alpha bunch below. Isn't there a way to get around that?"

Maggie scratched her head. "So . . . try the reset on the starwisp tellurion filter. That should make it work."

Kennedy reprogrammed and pressed the reset. "Yes! That did it!"

"Nice work," Cody said. "Through the GPS system I can send the coordinates on a secure hookup to my contact at the DOD."

"DOD? You mean we're dealing with the Department of Defense?"

"That's all I can tell you," Cody said. "Trust me, okay?"

"Yes, sir."

"Kennedy, here's a number I need you to call." Cody handed

her a written note.

She entered the number and pressed the call button. It rang three times.

"Hello, this is Ryan. I'm away from my phone until next week. Please leave your—"

"Never mind," Cody told Ken. "Try this other number."

This time, someone answered. It was a child. "Hello, this is Ram."

"Rammy, this is Uncle Cody."

"Uncle Cody! We thought you were dead! They said your plane went down off the coast of—"

"Rammy, I need to talk to your dad immediately! Immediately! Do you understand, son?"

"I don't know if, I mean cell service is non-existent off the Venezuelan coast. That's where they're searching for you. I've been calling him this morning."

"Okay, Ram. Is Sam home?"

"No. I can't keep up with my brother anymore. We communicate electronically mostly. What's so urgent? There might be one possibility, but it's iffy."

"Try it! Whatever it is, try it!"

"Okay, Uncle Cody! My dad doesn't know about this yet. It's a superluminal sterile holographic convertor. I developed it myself. Me and Sam have used it to contact each other whenever we—"

"Just try it, son. This is no time to stand on ceremony."

"Okay, stand by."

"So, it's like a face-o-gram?" Maggie asked.

"Not exactly," Ram said. "It's a way to reach someone without using any device."

"Okay, okay. Just give it a shot." Cody was getting antsy.

Maggie spoke up. "That sounds like a signal that seeks out someone's unique DNA profile. It uses holographic memory data and gamma conversion dryware to communicate without digital inputs or wireless signals."

"These phones aren't set up for that," Kennedy said.

"Okay, Uncle Cody. My dad's talking to me. Can you send me your unit's flare ratio, and its compatibility to a terraform space fountain?"

"Uh . . . what's that?"

"Wait!" Kennedy said. "Who is this?"

"I'm Rammy Maxwell. "Who's this? You sound cute!"

"Rammy, I need to know if you're using trans-human radonical connectors or just genetic plasma loops."

"I'm using the loops. You can just adjust your unit to a Stanford Tauros or a space elevator. That should put us on the same page."

Maggie interrupted. "But, Rammy, that'll only work if you have a built-in or downloaded psycho-history phaze neutralizer."

"*Sheese!* Good catch. I'm downloading one right now. Okay, you should be able to talk to my dad in about five seconds."

Both girls screamed, as suddenly the image of a man sitting in thin air outside the aircraft looked right at them and smiled. When he began to speak, they heard his voice loud and clear inside their headsets.

"Good to see you, Gunfighter. We all feared you were dead. Confirm your current position."

Maggie blurted out, "We're currently orbiting the 13th Parallel, 65.9661 west and—"

"Thank you, young lady. That's right in the very middle of the

Caribbean Sea. We were searching off the Venezuelan coast."

"Ryan, I'm gonna ask you to use classified technology. A lot of lives are at stake, and we're running out of time. Do you have your remote *Tommy John* satellite hookup with you?"

"Never leave home without it. You know that, Gunfighter."

"Awesome," Cody said. "You can access my GPS at port seventeen, Oscar-Delta-four-zero-niner-niner-eight. Pull up coordinates Alpha-one. I need an amphibious landing craft capable of evacuating about ninety people sent to those coordinates."

"Okay. It'll take about ten minutes. Anything else?"

"Affirmative. Access GPS coordinates Alpha-two. I need something at that location transferred to our barn at Houston. Tell Mom and Dad to alert the, uh, associates back in H-Town. The empty barn. They're gonna be surprised."

"Okay, what is this object?"

"You'll have to use your mag-inverted penetration viewer. You'll figure it out. It'll be the crowning *jewel* of your year, if you catch my drift."

"Got it," Ryan said. "All this should take place in the next thirty minutes."

"One more thing, Ryan. Can you collapse a Sabonic Cage Umbrella? It's directly below us."

"Hmmm, that's cutting-edge. It has to be a shield of some sort, right?"

"Affirmative. There is supposed to be an island below us."

"Got it! That's just a big light-bender. Gimme one minute."

"Much obliged, Ryan. Tell my big sis 'hi.' Gunfighter out."

Cody breathed a sigh. "Good job, ladies! Let's go get everybody off that island."

"Look!" Maggie said. "There's the island again! Look at all the smoke. You can hardly see the ground. Wait, what's that long highway down there?"

Cody looked down through his left window. "That's not a highway. That's a long airplane runway. We knew we'd find one somewhere. But we aren't going there now."

"The smoke's coming out of that mountain! That's scary!"

"I know, ladies. We need to expedite. Hang on."

Cody reduced the thrust and began to descend rapidly. He called Victor using one of the coms he had confiscated from a prisoner. He inadvertently left his aircraft headset on, allowing the girls to hear.

"Gunfighter to Deep Blue. Do you read me?"

"Affirmative, Gunfighter! I've been calling you. Pablo freed the other three prisoners, and they took Diamond. They forced her to go back to the other cave and lead them to the pirate treasure. I have my hands full with all these kids. They shot Thirsty Giant. He's alive but just holding on."

"How did Pablo know about the treasure?"

"He eavesdropped and heard you and Diamond talking about it. They stole one of the small boats from us. They plan to escape with Diamond and as much treasure as they can carry."

The two girls had become suddenly silent.

Cody banged his fist on the yoke. "It's my fault!" He covered his eyes and composed himself. "Ladies, we have to make one more stop."

21

GUNS OR ROSES

The De Havilland Beaver carried Cody and his two new female associates downward, circling and descending toward what would soon become a lava-scorched island. The sweet hum of the turbine engine did little to bring Cody's emotions under control. The Beaver had completed its mission. Almost.

Maggie and Kennedy seemed out of character sitting in silence as the aircraft circled the island and then began a long final approach to the south beach. The sight of Cody, the confident one, the steel-faced commander, now writhing for someone named Diamond and banging his hands on the yoke, had shocked their senses.

Cody glanced at Kennedy, sitting next to him in the cockpit, and forced a thin smile. She answered with an amiable shrug, and then chanced a question.

"Mr. Musket, may I ask who Diamond is? We can see that you care for her."

"Ever heard of Diamond Casper?"

Kennedy looked back at Maggie as their mouths dropped open. For a moment, the only sounds were the outside air streaming past the aircraft and the smooth engine holding a steady descent. They could see the sandy, flat beach below getting closer and closer as Cody pulled his Glock from his pocket to install a fresh, fully-loaded magazine.

"Do you women ever pray?" Cody asked. "Pray that I didn't get someone I care about hurt or . . . or worse. There's been enough pain for today. Some days it's roses. Some days it's guns. Today, it's guns."

Cody set the Beaver down with a soft nudge on the beach. He brought the aircraft to rest about 100 meters east of the cave. He could see Pablo's small boat pulled up on the sandy shore in the distance.

"You ladies must stay in this plane. Don't come out of here and don't let anyone see you. Move to the very back in the cargo area where there are no windows. I will be back for you in a few minutes."

As he trotted ahead toward a showdown with four killers, the wind kicked up from the south, bringing waves farther up onto the sand. Pablo's boat was beginning to skim around with each wave. The south wind was now blowing the smoke toward the other side of the island, clearing the air.

He looked back and noticed that the previously yellow Beaver was nearly solid black with ash and soot deposits from flying through the smoke. Funny how that worked. Flying at 150 miles per hour, smoke seemed to stick like a magnet.

Cody hoped he had parked the aircraft far enough away to catch the four abductors unaware. Against better judgment, he now allowed his thoughts to turn inward for one moment. Diamond had endured her share of abuse and heartbreak, and now his conversational indiscretion had put her squarely in the hands of four world-class abusers. Which would he be today? An evangelist, or an avenger?

Was he making a foolish decision? Four against one? If he failed to return, Maggie and Ken would be alone, vulnerable, and unprotected. If he had taken them to a place of safety first, it would have been too late to return and save Diamond. Should he have chosen which ones to save?"

No. This day wasn't about settling. This day was about finishing it. No one would be lost.

He stopped at the bottom of the hill and looked upward toward the broken-down cave entrance. His face burned as he caught sight of a white pullover blouse — one that he recognized — hanging from the opening. It was a signal — they were waiting for him. His SEAL survival training took over his mind. If he wanted to save her, he'd have to be the one with a clear head.

What were the four tangos thinking? So little time remained. The mountain was in travail, eruption was imminent, yet their thirst for revenge was stronger than their fear of death. Classic sociopathic rage — domination at any cost. What had they done to her? Was she even still alive?

His seething legs wanted to run straight up the slope with his weapon leading the way, but he wouldn't stand a chance.

Instead, he ran farther west along the shoreline until he came to a grassy slope from which he would be out of sight. He scrambled to the top, intending to make his way around to the back entrance, but the ground began to shake again — the rumbling, the steam rising from the reef, the sulfur smell. The shaking continued for several minutes, then ceased.

He hugged the side of the hill as he moved laterally back toward the front entrance. The shaking had loosened the rocks which had blocked the door.

He heard voices. Only two — Pablo and Diamond.

"I'm not leaving you here as a witness. If this place wasn't getting ready to explode, I would make grand sport of you right here! But you're going with me. Nobody's coming to save you! Let's go!"

"Don't you fear God at all, Pablo? You saw what happened to your associates. You're lucky to be leaving with your pants, especially with the way you've stuffed your pockets. Every child you've hurt will haunt your memory forever. And if we survive, you can be sure Cody will find us."

"Your boyfriend is dead."

Cody carefully moved closer until he was positioned about five meters away. He crouched out of sight near the jagged edge and waited. Then Pablo and Diamond appeared, his left arm pulling her through the opening, his right hand pressing a semi-automatic handgun against her temple. Pablo nervously scanned the beach for signs of trouble, proving he wasn't certain Cody was dead. Cody dared not make a move — too much risk of losing her forever. He prayed Pablo would not spot him.

That's when Cody saw something else that heightened the stakes. On the beach below, in plain sight, two blond girls stood motionless, trying to hold the hair out of their own faces as the strong south wind whistled over the beach and up the hill. They were frozen, their big eyes glued to the drama unfolding.

Pablo saw the girls. "What do we have here?" Pablo shouted. "Now we have a full crew! We will all go in the boat!"

Cody had worked his way carefully behind Pablo, but now Ken and Maggie had placed themselves in harm's way, defying his instructions. Where were Pablo's three associates? Why had they not appeared?

He had achieved what he had originally hoped — no one even knew he was there save the two airheads at the bottom of the hill. But with the gun barrel pressed against Diamond's head, he was still afraid to make a move.

Then, in a morning of surprises, the unexpected happened again.

"Go ahead! Make my day!"

Had Kennedy lost her mind completely? Now Cody's dilemma deepened. Pablo trained his weapon on the daring teenager. This was Cody's chance to save Diamond, but what about Ken at the bottom of the slope? His racing heart was in his throat.

So, God, don't let me have to choose who lives and who dies. For the kids, for Diamond . . . I'm in way over my head . . .

Suddenly Diamond's voice broke through the madness — sharp, smack, audacious.

"Pablo, honey, you ain't nothin' but a freakin' *invertebrate!*"

Her cheeky defiance clearly unnerved Pablo, causing his rage to finally explode. He jerked his head around and glared at her. *"Invertebrate??"*

"Dat means you a butt-ugly, cold-blooded animal wid no brain and no spine!"

Pablo drew back his pistol as if to strike Diamond in the face, but this gave Cody the opportunity he needed. He pounced like a king cobra, gripping Pablo's gun hand in mid-air, breaking the killer's wrist, separating him from his weapon, and hurling him headlong down the hill. Diamond lost her balance and slipped on loose rocks, sliding halfway down the slope.

Cody rushed to Diamond's aid. "Where are the other three? Are they still in play?"

She struggled to catch her breath. "No. No, they aren't. I can't really explain it."

He lifted her to her feet. "Can you walk?"

"I'm fine. I only skinned my knee." She shivered and crossed her arms as the airborne sea mist swirled right through her.

He put his arms around her. "For a minute, I thought . . ."

She read his face. "It's okay, sweetie, I'm fine. Really."

"C'mon. We need to move." He began helping her down the hill. "There's no time to get your blouse. It's stuck in the rocks up there at the cave."

"I'm fine with this bikini top."

"*Invertebrate?* Where'd that come from?"

"I don't know! It was the only thing I could think of!"

"*Ha!*" Cody huffed. "A heckuva risk!"

"A *diversion*, right? Something unexpected?" She breathed heavily. "So, who are these young ladies with you?"

"Kennedy's the talker. Maggie's the schemer. All the way from Kansas. My genius flight crew." He stared at the two bug-eyed, wind-blown figures. "And they may have saved your life."

Pablo lay moaning, trying to get up. "Why didn't you kill me?"

"You're only alive because my Glock jammed," Cody informed him. "Besides, we've had enough killing for one day. You should have left here a day ago, Pablo. You've sacrificed your life for revenge and greed, and you've just been outsmarted by a woman you've disrespected for the last time."

Pablo shuddered. "But you're dead! They told us you were dead. You will kill me now?"

"I'm not gonna kill you, Pablo. I'll just relieve you of those britches with the stuffed pockets, then you can be on your way. You'd better hurry. That little boat you snatched for yourself won't get you very far."

Pablo threw his boots and dungarees on the ground and then made a run for the boat. He pushed it into the water with his good hand, but the pounding waves overcame him, capsizing the boat.

"C'mon, ladies!" Cody shouted. "We need to expedite. Time's running out! Gotta get all my women onboard the aircraft."

"*All your women?*"

"Seems appropriate right now. You can slap me later."

Ken and Maggie stared like withering statuettes when they saw Diamond Casper coming toward them with ugly scrapes on her arms, faded jeans with new holes in the knees, and a muddy designer bikini top. She still had the stitches in her shoulder and bruises on her abdomen.

"Let's go!" Cody yelled again. "You girls are in deep trouble. I told you to say put! Here, carry these dungarees. We've got little time."

Kennedy reacted. "*Gross!* These pants reek!"

"Why are they so heavy?" Maggie wanted to know. "What's in these pockets?"

"No time to look." Cody rushed everyone along. "No time to explain. Let's keep moving."

Jogging back to the Beaver was a challenge. The wind had reached gale status, and the beach was now a foot deep in seawater. Diamond faltered, so Cody and Kennedy supported her.

Maggie fell face down, but did not let go of the dungarees. She fingered the bulging objects in the pockets, not knowing what they consisted of, obviously wondering what was so important that the bad guy would load himself down at such a time.

The nose of the Beaver was now facing out to sea, the gusts having turned the aircraft into the wind. The waves had become higher and higher, and the Beaver was bobbing and twisting.

They all climbed aboard. Maggie and Kennedy piled into the back seat while Cody helped Diamond buckle her safety belt up in the copilot chair. The fierce winds rocked the wings and swung the tail back and forth like a weather vane.

Cody started the engine, spooling up the whining turbine, then applied thrust, propelling the aircraft forward against the onslaught of an angry surf. The potent waves hammered against the floats, sending mist and foam into the air while the powerful Beaver cut its way into a forty-knot south wind. After several collisions with high-rolling waves, the Beaver lifted itself above the water and rode the wind to an altitude of about 100 feet.

Turbulence continued to rock the Beaver as Cody turned westward and followed the coastline back toward the cove where Victor had taken the small boats loaded with kids.

The two girls in the back reflected gloom, even horror on their faces. They forgot all about checking the pockets of the odorous dungarees, gripping each other as if to prevent being ripped apart by the herky-jerky movements of the airplane.

Diamond looked back for a brief moment, then smiled. "My name's Diamond, girls. Which one of you is which?"

Maggie and Kennedy seemed unable to answer at first, then both responded with their names.

"We're gonna be okay," Diamond assured. "God is with us, and we have a good pilot." Then she leaned toward Cody and said nothing, but her face spoke plainly enough — *"Do you have any idea how to get us off this island?"*

Cody spoke to the girls in the rear seat. "Ladies, we're headed Back toward the cove where I asked you to get me the first lat-long reading, remember?"

"Affirmative, sir," Maggie said.

Kennedy nodded.

"Good. So, when we get there, I'm hoping to see a boat large enough for everyone to get aboard."

Diamond looked at Cody incredulously. "A boat?" She turned around and glanced back. The two girls shrugged as if to say, "*We don't know what he's talking about either.*"

"Cody, honey, where is the boat coming from?"

"I'll fill in the details later. Right now, we have to secure the boat and get everyone on board. It's going to take all of us. It is a modern landing craft designed for military operations. How are you holding up back there, Ken? Maggie?"

"We're, uh, okay. We're sorry, Mr. Musket. Sorry for getting out of the plane earlier," Kennedy said.

"Yeah, we were really scared when the plane started shaking," Maggie added.

"We'll talk about that later. Just follow my instructions. Is that clear?"

"Yes, sir."

"Affirmative, sir."

Cody followed the beach as it turned northward, picking up speed in the turn because the strong south wind was now a tailwind. The secluded cove was straight ahead and coming up quickly. The aircraft raced past the designated coordinates, but the cove was empty. He looked in every direction, but saw only the turbulent, angry water.

Cody frowned. He could see Victor attempting to get all the kids out of the smaller boats. The strong surf threatened to smash them against the rocks with the terrified children aboard.

"Cody, where's the boat you talked about? Those tiny boats are too dangerous."

Cody turned the Beaver around into the wind and flew back toward the designated coordinates. Suddenly, everyone gasped. A boat had seemingly materialized out of thin air. It was sitting in the water near the secluded cove exactly as ordered.

But now another problem raised its head. The amphibious landing craft was drifting northward, the prevailing wind blowing it right past the intended docking point. If something did not happen quickly, the boat would simply float away.

"Cody! Why are they sailing away? Who's driving that boat?"

Cody cleared his throat. "Actually, there is no crew. I'll explain later. Right now, we need to recover that landing craft."

He called Victor on the com. "I'm coming in to drop my passengers. You and I gotta go after that boat."

"Copy that! Summa these kids are ready to assist getting your passengers off the plane. The leader among them is a thirteen-year-old kid named Joshua Scott. Does that ring a bell?"

Cody acknowledged, "Remember, he likes to be called *Josh*."

Cody made a right turn, circled back around, and turned into the wind once more for another approach toward the cove. It would be a tricky landing. If he were to lose the plane, all hope of recovering the wayward landing craft would be lost.

He spoke to his young helpers in the back. "Ladies, you've grown up today. I'm proud of you."

Cody set the Beaver down atop the waves, then began a slow turn toward the cove. He fought the winds until he was safely inside the cove, where the waters were smooth enough to finally breathe a momentary sigh of relief. As he approached the beach the kids tried to huddle close to the water, but Josh ushered them back to protect them from the propeller blades.

Cody taxied up onto the sand, then reached across Diamond

and opened her door. Several young men stood by to assist. One was clearly in charge. After the women were safely off the Beavor, Cody stretched his hand toward the young leader whose face was familiar. "Josh, I want to shake your hand. I'm glad you made it. I wanna tell you about your father later."

"I wanna go with you, sir. You might need help out there."

"That's not gonna happen, son. Now, listen up!" Cody handed Josh the com he had taken off one of the prisoners. "Wear this com. Before we return, Victor will instruct you how to get everyone ready to board the boat. We need a man in charge. Keep 'em calm 'til we return. That's an order. Now, make sure all stand clear. I'm gonna reverse the prop to push us back into the water."

"Yessir!"

As Cody reversed thrust, Diamond stood with arms around Ken and Maggie. They waved as Cody backed the plane away.

Cody scanned the huddling crowd. That's when he caught sight of one small boy separated from the rest. He couldn't see over the others, but had found his own spot. He stretched to catch a glimpse, and cupped his hands around his mouth shouting frantically. Cody couldn't hear him, but understand every word.

With menacing waters churning, perils lying in wait, the specter of little Freddy standing alone waving both arms in the air and screaming his lungs out brought Cody to an unlikely moment of serenity. He allowed himself to reflect upon the good things: Diamond Casper had become a prayer warrior, little Freddy had returned from the shadow of death, and Josh Scott was every bit the man his father had been.

For one golden moment, Cody smelled roses, *not* guns.

22

WILD AND CRAZY

Diamond's eyes were glued to the Beaver as Cody left the safety of the cove. She tried to see his face through the windshield, but the splashing surf and sea mist made it impossible.

"Who are all these kids?" Maggie wanted to know. "What's wrong with them? Didn't anyone feed them?"

"I'm not sure," Kennedy said, wiping saltwater off her face. "Some of them look sick."

"Those are the kids that you and Maggie would have been locked up with eventually," Diamond told them. "Some of these kids have been here for nearly a year. They'll need a long time to recover."

"How long do they keep you if you get sent here?"

"Maggie, sweetie, you don't get sent here. This place was run by bad people. That's why Cody and Victor had to . . . had to make sure they would never do this to children again."

Kennedy frowned. "You aren't like I thought you'd be, Diamond. I like you better this way."

"What way is that, Ken?"

"See, that's what I'm talking about. I told you my friends call me Ken, and you called me Ken."

"Your friend? Of course. Both of you are my friends."

"See there?" Kennedy said. "We never thought we'd actually meet you, and we never dreamed you'd be so . . . so much like a real person."

"Friends for life, right?" Diamond shivered.

"Yes, ma'am."

"That's right, ma'am."

Kennedy realized Diamond's arm felt cold. "Ma'am, maybe we can move farther back from the water." ·

Then a shirtless teenage boy approached, carrying his t-shirt. "Ma'am, would you like to wear my shirt?"

Diamond looked up in time to see three more young men offering their shirts. She politely thanked them and refused.

The selfless gesture moved the girls to tears. "That bikini top is really muddy," Maggie said. "And it doesn't look warm."

"You have scratches on your arms," Kennedy told Diamond. "I'm gonna ask that Josh dude if he knows where we can get a first-aid kit."

She got up and made her way through the crowd. What she saw stifled her. The critically ill younger children were all together in one area. Three had bites on their legs and feet. Teeth marks were clearly visible, the bites red, enflamed. One was vomiting and looked emaciated. She wanted to turn away, but kept going. Diamond needed first-aid.

When she finally spotted Josh near the shallow water on the other side of the cove, she called out to him. "Josh! Do you have a first-aid kit?" She moved toward him.

He was tall and wiry with passionate gray eyes. His dark hair was long and unkempt, his fair skin splashed with saltwater. Before he could respond to her, a powerful concussion rattled the ground. This time, the explosive rumble was deafening, giving way to an escalating roar, and the violent shaking seemed to worsen with every passing second.

Smoke came swirling into the cove, defying the winds by moving in the opposite direction and hugging the water. The children screamed, their cries ignored by the powerful forces that threatened to bring the world down on top of them.

Kennedy fell into the shallows and could not get up. An undertow began pulling her toward the open sea like a hungry monster from the deep. She tried to grip the bottom, hoping to halt her slide, but the slippery sand went through her fingers. When she tried to yell for help, she swallowed a mouthful of water.

Just then, she felt two strong hands take hold under her arms. She coughed and gasped for breath as she noticed two big feet attached to two lanky legs back pedaling with her toward the dry shore. Finally, he let go.

"Can you breathe?" the person shouted. "I was getting your first-aid kit when I saw you fall in the water."

She rolled onto her back and looked up, but he was gone. Then she spotted a small boy sitting on the ground crying.

"Mr. Cody! Mr. Cody!"

Kennedy crawled to the child and put her arms around him. "*Shhhh.* Do you know Cody too? He's my friend and he'll be back. *Shhhh.* What's your name, little guy?"

The boy had dark hair with sharp brown eyes and round cheeks. He was soaked through and through, shivering. "My name is Freddy. Freddy Reyes. Mr. Cody always goes away. When will he come back?"

Maggie and Diamond struggled against the quaking ground,

huddling with a pile of screaming children. "This'll be over soon."

But Diamond's assurance seemed hollow in the midst of such uncontrolled earth palpitations.

Maggie was still clutching Pablo's dirty dungarees. She had repeatedly ignored the temptation to look inside the pockets, but Cody had said to keep up with them, and she had done just that.

During the shaking, she spotted an unfortunate victim, an unexpected bystander fighting for life near the base of a rock on the edge of the cove. It was a single, long-stemmed red rose. The tremoring ground had caused the head of the rose to repeatedly strike the rock, bruising the petals and knocking some to the g.

She freed herself from Diamond's grasp and crawled to the rescue. When she returned, she slipped the battered rose into the only unoccupied pocket of the pants.

"I want to give this to Cody," she said.

The violent tremors continued. The air became noticeably warmer. The smoke yielded larger ashes, and the hot sulfur smell made the kids cough. The winds shifted, sending black swirlwinds humming and circling across the waves. Even the wind did not know which way to run.

~   ~   ~

Cody and Victor had to chase the landing craft over five miles before they could devise a way to get Victor aboard. After that, Victor would be forced to manually operate the craft in rough seas and execute an amphibious landing in a confined area. It would have been a challenge for the usual four-man crew, but with only one operator it could prove beyond difficult.

Cody had elected to not become airborne after departing the cove because the tailwind would have created excessive landing speed, making it extremely hazardous to set the plane down again in the crowning waves. He simply added enough power to pull the Beaver over the water at a few knots faster than the boat. The Beaver was now reduced to a boat with wings.

But once they had pulled alongside the landing craft, they realized that an attempt by Victor to step from the floating Beaver directly to the boat would be out of the question. The seas were too rough, and the wing kept the aircraft at a twenty-foot arm's length, meaning that Victor would be forced to dive into the water and attempt to board the landing craft with no one on the vessel to pull him up. Without proper boarding gear and the help of another, that would likely be a fatal mistake.

"I have one idea," Cody said. "It's wild and crazy, and it's never been tried. So I'll leave it to you, since you're the one who'll have to make the jump."

"Jump?" Victor tightened his jaw, then grinned. "Wild and crazy? That's never stopped you before."

Cody nodded, and bit his lip. He prayed his wild and crazy scheme would not get his friend killed. But what choice did they have? He told Victor his plan, which involved some dangerous and tricky precision flying on a less than ideal day, and a daring jump from the aircraft to the boat.

"Okay, Gunfighter. I'm game. I have one question. Why didn't a crew show up with this boat?"

"It's classified. Trust me, Vic, I'd tell you if I could."

"Let me guess. Your brother-in-law with the DOD is able to transfer solid objects inter-dimensionally with satellite support, but cannot transfer living human tissue, right?"

Cody grimaced. "I have no idea what you're talking about."

Victor tightened his life vest. "I just wanna say I've been on two airplane rides with you and I haven't enjoyed myself either time."

"Yep, you never know who you'll meet on a plane these days."

"Ain't that the truth!" Vic rolled his eyes toward the bobbing boat . "Now, finally, we get to do something fun."

They both instinctively looked toward the island. Lightning bolts now electrified the air and the mountain was erupting. Huge puffs of gray smoke exploded into the upper reaches, intermingling with fast-moving black clouds overhead. Bits of flaming magma shot forth like Roman candles. Even from five miles away, the scene made them wonder if anyone at the cove would still be alive when and if they returned.

Cody and Victor bore down on their mission. Cody applied thrust and lifted the Beaver a few feet above the water. He flew on a northeasterly course until they were about a half mile from the boat, then turned left and circled back toward the landing craft on a 30 degree intercept angle, flying into the face of a forty-knot headwind.

Victor pulled the door pins and let the passenger door fall into the water. He released his safety belt and stepped onto the float below the door, then waited.

With most of the fuel used up, the stall speed of the Beaver was 50 knots. If Cody could keep the airspeed at 55 knots, the aircraft would not stall, and the 40-knot headwind would slow the aircraft to a speed of only 15 knots relative to the water. Add the speed of the boat at 5 knots, and that would mean an intercept speed of only 20 knots — a marginal, but viable plan.

"Okay, Vic, we got one shot at this. Boat intercept is in thirty seconds."

As the pitching boat neared, Cody maneuvered directly over the bow.

"For the kids!" Victor yelled, stepping off the float of the Beaver. He landed on the deck and rolled to break his fall. Perfect execution.

Cody's exuberance ended when the aircraft suddenly fell from beneath him. The left float caught a railing on the boat which spun the Beaver around and sent it plunging tail-first off the port side.

Cody rolled out of the cockpit beneath the troubled waters, then popped his head above the surface and signaled thumbs-up. Victor yanked off his life vest and threw it to Cody, then gave him a lifeline and pulled him aboard.

As Cody stood on the deck dripping wet and out of breath, he glanced again at the mountain. The smoke was now backing up, hiding most of the island from view. The winds had changed.

"You look wet, Gunfighter. Let's go below and try to figure out how to start the engines on this floating boxcar."

The men gained control of the boat and began sailing back toward the island. The engines whined at high speed and propelled the landing craft at 15 knots with the bow pitching up and down like a seesaw. In twenty-five minutes, they turned into the cove to the cheers of everyone, and coasted onto the sand.

Josh Scott, having received instructions from Victor, had just informed everyone that Cody and Victor would be arriving with the boat. He kept everyone out of the way until the boat was secured and the front ramp was opened. There was no time to waste.

"The injured go on first," Josh yelled. "They'll be taken to the rear, where medical supplies will be found. That area is designated *Sick Bay*."

"The next group will be children under the age of seven. The third group to board will be everyone else. If you do not know your age, take a good guess." His deep eyes and assertive voice calmed the fearful chatter.

"After you are aboard, sit in one of the seats and fasten your safety belt. There will be a life vest under your chair. If you do not know how to put it on, ask for help. No panic, but we gotta expedite, people!"

In light of the urgency and confusion, thirteen-year-old Josh Scott had been the voice of confidence needed. Cody and Victor had depended on him to step up. He did.

Maggie and Diamond noticed that during Josh's remarks, Kennedy worked her way close to him and would not take her eyes off him.

After everyone was aboard, they closed the ramp and prepared to churn backward off the sand and make a run for the open sea.

Lightning flashed from cloud to cloud while smoke and floating ash brought on an eerie darkness.

Finally, just as the boat pushed off the sand, the ground shook so violently that rocks began to slide from the surrounding hills down on to the beach. It took only a few seconds for the cove to become a pile of rocky rubble as the boat slipped away with 92 souls aboard.

23

THE ROSE

There was no instruction manual on how to escape from an island intent on destroying itself by fire and water. As the escapees were tossed about in the amphibious landing craft, it seemed as though all the elements had collided, forming a perfect storm from which there was no way out.

In the first few minutes of their voyage, they were pummeled with black ice stones from high-level thunderstorms — black because of the soot in the air. The lightning bolts were not visible because of the smoke and ashes which had created early-afternoon darkness, but the nebulous flashes followed by thunderous explosions drew terrified screams from most of the kids.

The landing craft had two decks. The lower deck was only five feet in height, but most of the children could stand up. At least they were not as exposed as they would have been in an older vintage landing craft.

Cody and Victor kept an eye peeled for the barrier reef. The low visibility made them reluctant to cruise more than 7 knots. They decided to head north toward Puerto Rico, a distance of about three hundred miles. The boat, cruising at a depth of only four feet when fully-loaded, had not run aground earlier when it had drifted north of the reef, so it made sense that north would be a safe route of escape.

The boat continued to pitch up and down and roll side to side. Many of the kids were nauseated. When the air began to clear, Victor called out another warning sign to Cody.

"Look at this!" Victor pointed to something in the water.

Cody came over for a look. The water was bubbling. The sulfur smell was overwhelming.

They looked toward the island three miles behind them. The mountain was still in full eruption mode. They could see an orange glow reflecting through the scattered clouds, and red-hot lava flowing down from the peak. The ice pellets had ceased but the rain continued to pelt the deck of the boat, and distant thunder rumbled through the sky like a million stallions.

The sulfur odor and the bubbling water made Victor's heart race. "I wish I had your faith. You'd better pray this bubbling doesn't mean the ocean is gonna turn into a bath of hot magma!"

At that moment, Diamond came up the steps to the top deck. "I've never seen a volcano." She still wore the bikini top, but had found blankets below and had wrapped one around herself.

"Here are a couple of blankets for you guys," she said, handing them each one. "The rain's cold. You gotta be freezing."

All of a sudden, an orange fountain of molten lava burst into the air about 100 meters behind the boat.

"Get below! Everybody get below!" Victor shouted.

They scrambled down the steps and closed the hatch. Screams and cries from the children filled the already-tense air.

They waited an hour before opening the hatch again. The rain had ceased. The air had cleared of smoke, and the island was visible again.

Was it time to relax?

They increased their speed to 14 knots. The late afternoon winds had died down and the water was calm.

Cody walked below again. Freddy was waiting for him at the bottom of the steps. When the child reached up to him, Cody wearily lifted him off the floor.

"I knew you would come back, Cody Musket. Mama Diamond said no weapon could hurt you. I hope you don't leave again."

Cody was too weary to notice that he had caught everyone's attention the minute he had arrived. He held the child close and began whispering in the boy's ear. Diamond stood near enough to sense that Cody's emotions were testing his limits. He was wound up tighter than a hang noose.

When he finally set Freddy down, the boy was smiling. Maggie and Kennedy wanted to talk to him, but Diamond stepped in. "Ladies, this man has already had a long day. He's exhausted. I need to put him to bed."

Cody didn't argue. She led him to a bunk near the stern. Some of the guys had placed blankets down for him.

"I need to see Parker. I heard he was shot."

"He's asleep. We finally got him pain meds here on the boat. I doubt he'll make it. Pablo shot him in the upper chest."

"Can you explain to me what happened to Pablo's three henchmen at the cave? Why didn't they come out to fight?"

She spoke softly. Most of the kids were listening. "Pablo loaded his pockets with jewels from the pirate stash, so the other three went down there. They started shouting that the jewels were no longer there. The entire treasure had disappeared, so they said. Then we heard them yelling for help, and the whole place shook. That was it."

Cody showed no expression. He knew more than he let on, but she had become accustomed to it. She wasn't about to ask.

He removed his wet shirt and wrung it out. "A helicopter is supposed to arrive in the morning. Medical supplies, food, a doctor."

"That's wonderful. How long to Puerto Rico?"

"About twenty-eight hours, give or take. Too bad there isn't a hot shower on board. This isn't exactly a cruise ship. I need to at least get outta these wet clothes. I guess you figured out I crashed the plane."

"You're always crashing something, and you're always needing your clothes dried out. Here, get under the blanket. Hand me your shirt and pants. I'll hang 'em up to dry. We, uh . . . have an audience here, you know."

"Seems like this is getting old." Cody pulled up the blanket.

"I have to tell you something, Cody. That little Maggie has carried those dirty dungarees with her everywhere. She even brought them on board. She hasn't looked at what's inside the pockets, but the curiosity is killing her. She also has a surprise for you. She took a risk to get it before I could stop her."

"What sort of surprise?"

"I'm not going to ruin the surprise. She can hardly wait . . . Uh, Cody? Cody, are you still awake?"

Cody slept well until after sundown. None of the children slept a wink. Everyone was tired and hungry, but no one wanted to sleep.

Cody arose and wrapped the blanket around himself. He then walked by the children and greeted them all. Some reached out to touch him as he passed, while others showed no life in their eyes. He slowly walked up the steps and set foot on the deck.

Diamond was sitting alone near the bow listening to the sea ripple smoothly past the boat. The motors were humming in sync. The half-moon had risen in a clear sky. The glow of molten lava spewing from the mouth of the volcano sixty miles off the stern created an eerie sense of irony. From here the volcanic wonder of nature was beautiful, calm, serene. Up close, it had been the nature of Hell itself, as though someone had opened the gates.

"I've been waiting for you," she told him. "I hung your clothes here so they would dry faster in the breeze. They're nearly dry if you wanna put 'em on."

While he put on his shirt and dungarees, she looked up at the moon. "Do you think anyone will ever live up there? On the moon?"

"Why do you ask me that?"

"Well, Mr. Gunfighter, I was just wondering what it would be like to start the human race over somewhere else. Like, would there eventually be evil again like we see on this planet, or would it be all good?"

"It depends on who you start over with."

"Cody, you had a day to remember. This day will be forever etched in the mind of every child. I knew you were coming back. I knew nothing would touch you."

"How did you know that?"

She put her arms around his neck. "Do you remember when I told you I had prayed to God for the first time?"

He sighed. "I do remember. You said you weren't sure if God had even paid attention, or something like that."

"I said I had asked Him to reveal Himself to me, but that nothing had happened. Then I told you I had dreamed something really crazy. The dream was about riding in a black airplane with two blond teenage girls. That made no sense at the time."

A smile crept across his weary face. "I barely remember that."

"So, when I got into that plane today and looked back and saw Ken and Maggie, I remembered the dream."

"But the Beaver was yellow."

"Not after you got through flying around in all that soot. The plane was almost completely black. That's when I knew God had heard me, and I knew this would be a day of beating the odds."

Cody turned and stood by the rail, looking over the side of the boat at the gentle wake that rippled in the moonlight. He put his hand over his face.

"When I saw those sixty kids in that . . . that holding cell . . . the dark, the cold, hungry, some dying . . ." He stopped to breathe deeply. "I mean, my dad once tried to explain what happens in your head when so much sorrow and so much anger take over your mind at the same time. Today, I found out. I . . . I let it affect me. I let a good man die. Scott . . . he pushed Vic and me aside and took on six men alone. I'm alive because he died instead of me. Angel's dead, Jesse Flores killed, Parker's hurt. Why am I still walking around?"

Cody did not know that Maggie and Ken had followed him to the deck, and that they were listening in the shadows. Ken had brought little Freddy with her, and most of the other kids had decided to follow.

Diamond noticed the audience. She moved toward Cody who was still staring over the side of the boat and put her hands on his shoulders. "So, isn't there a Bible verse which says that some days you should kick ass, and other days you heal people?"

Cody spit into the water, then chuckled. "Well . . . not exactly in those words, but Ecclesiastes says that everything has its season, including a time to heal and time to kill."

"Cody, you need to turn around." She gently turned him. "Look at all these children. Look at their happy faces. Yesterday, they had no hope. They needed somebody with enough faith and . . . and enough love to change the odds. Yesterday, they needed an avenger. Today, they need an evangelist. Your job isn't finished."

Maggie had waited long enough. "Mr. Musket, I found something in a corner of the cove growing all alone. I want to give it to you."

Cody offered her a ragged smile. "Okay, Maggie. Diamond said you had something for me." His hard eyes softened. "I been waitin' to see it."

She held up Pablo's smelly dungarees and reached into one of the pockets. "I put it in here so I wouldn't lose it."

She pulled out the wounded rose that she had carried through hell in a pair of dirty dungarees. The petals were crushed. The stem was broken.

"This is for you, Mr. Musket. You said it in the plane, remember? Some days, guns. Some days, roses."

Cody dropped to one knee and wrapped Maggie in his arms. His trapped feelings, the stress of leadership, his grief for fallen friends in a battle he did not choose. His shoulders began to shake with emotions hidden in his deepest soul. When Diamond lost her composure, the children became hushed and tearful, but the poignant moment soon transformed into a celebration.

Cody looked into the eyes of the soft-spoken thirteen-year-old. "I heard you took a risk to bring me this, Maggie. This is no small thing you have done." He stood and lifted the rose for everyone to see. "For all of us, and . . . for those we've lost . . . for those who bravely sacrificed their lives to bring us this moment, yeah . . . we're going home. This is a day for roses."

He presented the rose to Diamond. She held tightly to the rose while he kissed her, and kissed her, and kissed her.

The children mumbled, then applauded. Kennedy, still holding Freddy, came near and nudged Cody.

He turned around. "You're a loose cannon, child." He paused. "And I wouldn't have it any other way. But I gotta say, if I were your dad I wudda grounded both of you for getting' outta that plane."

The two girls straightened their faces and exchanged a long glance.

Maggie's vocal cords were barely audible. "We don't have a dad."

"So, your mother is a single mom, and she's afraid to fly?"

"We don't have a mom either." Kennedy's voice quiet as a feather. "Maggie and I are the ones afraid to fly."

"You both did just fine today," Diamond said. "So how do you feel about flying now?"

Kennedy wrinkled her nose. "After flying with Cody? Are you kidding?"

"Yeah," Maggie said, "*never again!*"

Cody folded his arms. "So, if you don't have a mom and didn't steal her car like you said, what's the real reason you ended up on that island?"

Both girls stood tight-lipped. Finally, Ken decided to end the charade.

"It was Mr. Carpenter's car I stole. My third different foster dad. He was mean to me, so I drove his car to Garden City to pick up Maggie."

Maggie further explained. "You see, we were in two separate homes. Ken picked me up, but a Kansas State Trooper arrested us and drove us in a van with some other kids to Kansas City. Then this judge sentenced us."

"Yeah," Kennedy said. "After that, they flew us to some far away airport near the ocean, then made us get on this nasty old boat that took us to that island. We didn't even know how many years our sentence was."

"*What?*" Cody winced. "You girls weren't arrested. You were abducted. How long ago was that?"

"Thirty-two days."

Diamond took Cody's arm. "I think Mr. Parker is awake. He was asking for you a few minutes ago. He wants to see us both."

Cody nodded. They began making their way below to Parker's bedside. Diamond lowered her voice. "By the way, Mr. Parker and Tige had a rather lengthy discussion while you were asleep."

"What about?"

"Not sure, but Tige has not left his bedside since."

They approached the bed and Cody placed his hand on Parker's arm.

"My time has come, Cody." Parker's voice low and raspy. "I see that God has graced you with marvelous young associates who need parents."

"How did you know they didn't have parents?" Diamond asked.

"I'm Thirsty Giant. I'm supposed to know." Parker swallowed hard and chuckled. "Cody, here's a hand-written document I created earlier today." He wheezed. "It makes you the soul trustee of . . . of all assets associated with my company. My two associates in Barcelona, Venezuela are named here. They will complete the transfer and . . ."

"Save your strength, Joe. Get some rest. We can discuss this when we get back to civilization."

"Lemme see your hands, both of you," Parker said.

Cody and Diamond joined their hands with his.

"What God has joined . . . let no man . . . put asunder . . . Amen."

The death of Thirsty Giant saddened everyone. There was a stillness, the acknowledgement that a rare soul was making his flight to Heaven. The soft hum of the motors, the gentle parting of the waters as the boat cut its way toward a peaceful harbor with 92 souls aboard.

"Greater love has no man . . ." Cody said quietly. "I'll see you on the other side, my friend."

In the quietness, someone was crying softly. He looked up to see Tige standing at the foot of the bed. She offered Cody a bittersweet smile with a tearful nod.

Cody turned around holding Diamond's hand and allowed himself a safe smile. He picked up Freddy with his free arm, then connected eye-to-eye with Ken and Maggie. "No more stealin' cars, ladies."

"Now what?" Diamond leaned against him and looked into his tired blue eyes.

Cody breathed a deep sigh of relief.

"Let's all go home."

The next instant, several older children began screaming on the upper deck. Something was wrong. Cody and Victor raced up the steps to investigate.

The commotion came from near the stern, where a crowd

had gathered. The kids were jumping up and down, yelling and pointing.

When Victor and Cody arrived, they aimed a flashlight in the direction the kids were pointing. They could not believe their eyes. Gripping the retaining rail on the side of the boat were two hands larger than iron beach balls with hairy fingers long enough to fit around a grown man's head.

When Cody looked over the side of the boat, he discovered that the hands belonged to a monster of a gorilla. The giant animal stared back at Cody and then pulled himself up and onto the deck, causing Victor and Cody to back up, giving this guy plenty of room.

The gargantuan beast must have pulled at least twenty gallons of saltwater on board with him as he came straight out of the ocean dripping wet and water-logged. He stood to a height of nearly ten feet, beating his chest and yelling. His wild eyes blinked excessively, perhaps irritated by the salty water, and maybe because of the bubbling up of the sulfur earlier. How long had he held onto the side of the boat? How long had it been since he had eaten?

Cody and Victor began pulling the children back, afraid of what was getting ready to happen. They recognized the giant ape. It was Godzilla the Third, the crafty anthropoid that had given Cupertino the slip.

Then as if there had not been enough surprises for one day, the children came running from all points and began crowding around the magnificent animal, calling out, "Godzilla! Godzilla!"

The large beast sat on the deck, his eyes soft and endearing as he allowed the children to sit in his lap and climb upon his great shoulders.

Having endured so much, the kids now frolicked around a lost friend who, like them, had been in a cage.

They had put over sixty miles between themselves and the island. Now the last survivor had finally come aboard.

"Gunfighter, how are we gonna get this beast off this boat? I mean, he looks even bigger here than on the island."

"Tell me something I don't already know. I guess a little genetic experimentation goes a long way these days."

Diamond finally stepped up next to Cody. "Look how sad his eyes are just since you guys have started discussing his fate."

"Yeah. I wonder how many kids he saw die on that island."

"I wonder what else he's seen," Victor added.

The creature made sharp eye contact with Cody. He couldn't speak any human languages, but the message in his suddenly menacing eyes was plain enough: "I'm coming with you."

~ ~ ~

11 p.m. the next evening, the final hours of the voyage

The lights of San Juan had finally come into view, flickering faintly in the distance. The voyage from X-ray Island had lasted thirty hours, and they were scheduled to dock at 2 a.m.

Normally the sight of land would have solicited cheers of joy from everyone, but most of the exhausted children were bedded down. Everyone was stuffed after a full meal. A few older kids had utilized a makeshift shower which recycled the water throughout the day. They also helped bathe some of the younger ones.

Two transport helicopters from Saint Vincent had brought

food, drinking water, medicine, a doctor, fresh clothing, and toiletry items such as soap and shampoo that morning. Children in greatest need had been taken aboard and flown to a hospital.

Another helicopter had arrived for the gigantic gorilla. Four animal experts had tranquilized the gentle beast, had loaded him into a padded cage, and had flown him to a wildlife preserve in the Lesser Antilles.

Cody and Diamond had taken most of the day to rest and had finally rinsed the salt, sand, and soot out of their hair. As the afternoon had progressed, Diamond observed that Cody had become moody again. The nearer to their destination, the more melancholia he displayed.

Moments before midnight, they stood alone on the bow watching the smooth water reflect in the scant moonlight.

"So, Mr. Cody, just Cody, you said we should all go home. What exactly did you mean? Where exactly is home? Houston? Or, do you seek refuge wherever the wind takes you?" She ran her fingers over his cheek. "You need a shave by the way. I guess you know that."

"So, you think I should shave before I take refuge?"

"Oh, it wouldn't hurt."

He locked his tired eyes on her face. "It fits."

"What fits?"

"The name, Sweet Ebony."

"Oh, is that my codename?"

His blue eyes saddened. "I've had time to think during the past twenty-four hours."

"I can see that," she whispered. "You have another mission. You're going alone to Barcelona to meet with Thirsty Giant's associates so you can complete the transaction and integrate his organization with yours."

He nodded. "I wanna take some people I love, but it's too dangerous."

"And just who would those people be?"

He held her shoulders. "I think you know."

"Oh, you mean *moi?* And what about your two blond teenage car thieves from Kansas and your five-year-old Panamanian swimmer?"

"I want to take 'em home with me, but . . ."

"I know, Gunfighter. You're like the passing clouds, always on the go to who knows where. It's always dangerous, and it's always urgent."

"I've already explained it to them. Mom and Dad will meet us in Puerto Rico. Planned Childhood will find good homes for them."

"Mr. Parker held our hands and said something about what God has joined together. Did that mean anything special, or . . . official?"

Cody cleared his throat. "We just gotta figure out how to make all the pieces fit." He forged a delicate smile, but he could not hide his feelings.

Diamond's soft raven curls swayed easily in the warm Caribbean breeze. Her wistful eyes like ebony pearls were troubled and silent. She had never known love before, but somehow, she knew this was the moment when love either speaks or forever holds its peace.

"I have seen flashes of joy in your eyes, Cody. But mostly, I see sadness. You're haunted by suffering children, especially the ones you can't save from the garbage bins, and the others that you can't be there to rescue. You're a victim too, Cody, because you cannot take the time to let somebody love you, to give you babies of your own. Is that part of your calling, or shouldn't you also be whole?"

"It won't always be this way," Cody breathed with a lumbering sigh. "So, are you headed home to Malibu for a while?"

"Actually, Global Direct Motion Pictures wants to start filming *Land Without Shame* on location in Venezuela in three weeks. I haven't decided yet. I suppose that's where I'll be, unless . . ."

"Maybe people will take you seriously for a change."

"That makes no difference now. I have the same vocabulary I've always had, but my definitions have changed. Five days staring death in the face and seeing my own reflection . . ." She shook her head. "Discovering who Jesus is . . . I mean, something's different inside me that I can't explain. Not yet, anyway."

"I should be finished in Barcelona in a couple of weeks," Cody offered.

"So, what then? Your work is important, and it never stops, right?"

"I wish I had a better answer," he said.

"So, I'll go to Venezuela and do the film. Cupertino is dead and his organization is in chaos. The film might just finish them off."

Cody lowered his tone. "It's a dangerous country."

"Cody, I will probably spend the rest of my life in the most dangerous hotspots on the planet."

"Why do you say that?"

"Because that's where I will most likely run into you." She kissed him on the cheek. "I'm tired. I'm going to get some sleep."

Her abrupt departure stunned him. Was she right? Was he a victim? As he watched her walk away leaving him standing alone, a sudden panic took him. It pulsed through his veins like fire.

"Wait." Cody put his hands into his front pockets.

Diamond turned around and stood quietly for a moment, then spoke passionately. "I can read your face from here, Cody Musket. It tells me that those three kids are tearing your soul apart. They aren't just *any* kids. Those three have marched right into the battle with you."

Cody deliberated, then walked slowly, nervously across the deck and eased his arms around her. "And, how 'bout you, Sweet Eb? Wavin' a flare in that monsoon? And that stunt you pulled on Pablo, makin' yourself a target to protect two girls you'd never laid eyes on?" He smiled circumspectly. "I hardly recognize you anymore. All the Musket women seem to have it."

"And?"

"And you . . . you have a way of saying things . . . Especially when you aren't acting."

"And?"

"And, if you're so bull-headed and determined to return to Venezuela, I'm comin' with you. Like I said, it's dangerous over there."

"So, how does a girl like me become, as you say, a 'Musket woman?'"

"You're either born a Musket or you marry someone in the family."

She felt her gut trembling like the distant island when it was ready to explode, fire and rain in her eyes, her lips next to his. "So then . . . maybe there's a chance for me?"

He kissed her, then whispered, "I've been a moron."

She shook him by his shoulders. "Kiss me again."

For five-year-old Freddy and two Kansas car thieves staked

out on the midships observation deck, the moment was perfect. Their tiny whispers were barely audible.

"What're Cody and Mama Diamond doing? I never see that before."

"*Shhh!* They're kissing, doh-doh head!"

"Yeah, in the moonlight and everything."

"Does that mean Mr. Cody and Mama Diamond want us?"

"*Ha!* I told you she would make him change his mind!"

The three children quietly bumped knuckles and high fived. A wide beam from Cody's flashlight caught them in the act.

"Okay, you kids, come out of there . . . *Now!*"

"Cody Musket, you have made me the luckiest . . . I mean the *most blessed* woman in the world! Do I get a codename? What about a callsign? Cody?"

Cody, with one hand over his face, "Oh, Lord help us!"

The End

Turn this page for a personal word from Author James N. Miller.

I'm James Miller. Thank you for reading the Muskets' story! Becoming a writer wasn't even on my bucket list, but after retirement from the business world my life became too quiet, the inactivity unbearable. That's when I began asking God for new direction and new creativity.

Now, I am age 71 with a four-part novel series that I can leave as a legacy of faith for my grandchildren. What a surprise! What a blessing!

After all the years, I have concluded that there are two lies which will rob you of your destiny—two lies you should guard yourself against:

(1) Your life can never be extraordinary. (2) God is predictable.

An extraordinary life is one lived in sweet companionship and in submission to the Holy Spirit, because that life is a daily supernatural walk that others will notice.

God never changes, but His nature is to be unpredictable. He is the God of surprise, and His creativity knows no bounds. I've seen real miracles, but seldom have I seen God do things the way I expected.

If you will walk with God, prepare to be surprised. Extraordinary things lie within you that only He can bring out, but, as Cody Musket might say, "You gotta cut the Almighty some slack. He does things His way. He's gotta style of His own. He's in a class by Himself." So smile . . .

www.facebook.com/nopitsodeep
Email James Miller: codymusket@gmail.com

Made in the USA
Middletown, DE
25 May 2019